Once upon a time, there were three very different little girls who grew up to be three very different women. But they have three things in common.

They're brilliant.

They're beautiful.

And they work for me.

My name is Charlie.

D1222022

CHARLIE'S ANGELS™

**Novelization by Elizabeth Lenhard
based upon the screenplay written by
Ryan Rowe and John August**

POCKET BOOKS
New York   London   Toronto   Sydney   Singapore

This book is a work of fiction. Names, characters, places and incidents are products of the author's imagination or are used fictitiously. Any resemblance to actual events or locales or persons, living or dead, is entirely coincidental.

An *Original* Publication of POCKET BOOKS

POCKET BOOKS, a division of Simon & Schuster, Inc.
1230 Avenue of the Americas, New York, NY 10020

TM & © 2000 Columbia Pictures Industries, Inc.
All rights reserved.

Motion Picture Photography © 2000 Global Entertainment
Productions GmbH & Co. Movie KG

ISBN: 0-7434-1023-8

First Pocket Books printing November 2000

10 9 8 7 6 5 4 3 2 1

POCKET and colophon are registered trademarks
of Simon & Schuster, Inc.

Printed in the U.S.A.

For Lacey

CHARLIE'S ANGELS™

PROLOGUE

October 16, 4:23 P.M.
Location: Virgin Air Flight #319; Altitude: 40,000 feet
Status: Lavatory occupied

Mr. Jones stood in the cramped coach-class rest room and gazed into the mirror. He adjusted the folds of his voluminous kente-cloth dashiki. He peered at his face—medium brown skin, carefully trimmed three days' growth of beard to add a touch of maturity to his youthful looks, and a serious scowl to offset his killer dimples. Mr. Jones was probably the best-looking guy on this plane.

He reached up to straighten the flat-topped cap on his short Afro. Then Mr. Jones walked out and made his way toward the front of the plane.

As he stepped into the first-class cabin, he felt ten pairs of eyes bore into him. Businesspeople looked up from their PowerBooks to eye him curiously. Fashionistas munching on fresh-baked cookies checked out his threads. And one shifty-eyed interloper in black gaped at him.

What? Mr. Jones thought. You people never saw a

six-foot-plus man in full African regalia in first class before?

Apparently not.

"I'm sorry, sir," came a nervous voice. Mr. Jones looked down to see a male flight attendant gently stopping him in his tracks. "This cabin is restricted to first cl—"

"Is this what you're looking for?" Mr. Jones asked in a deep, rumbling voice. He reached beneath the folds of his dashiki and whipped out a ticket.

The attendant examined the ticket, his head cocked at a curious angle. Mr. Jones lifted one eyebrow and prepared a glare. He flinched just slightly as the Fasten Seat Belts sign lit up with a little chime. This could get ugly real quick, he thought. I might just have to . . .

The flight attendant looked up and nodded warmly at Mr. Jones. "The captain would like passengers to take their seats and buckle up," the man said. "Is there anything I can get for you?"

Glare unnecessary. Curt politeness would do.

"Scotch and soda—hold the Scotch," Mr. Jones ordered, striding past the attendant with a grace that defied his imposing frame. "Pronto."

The attendant scurried to the galley. Mr. Jones stalked up the aisle. He paused at the emergency exit row and glanced down at the man in black, the shifty-eyed one with beads of sweat on his upper lip and a bobbling knee. The guy shot Mr. Jones a look and nodded nervously.

Pasqual, I presume, Mr. Jones thought. It was all

he could do not to roll his eyes. *This* was Pasqual? Mad bomber Pasqual? South Africa's scourge? Pshaw.

With a stony face, Mr. Jones planted himself in the aisle seat, next to Pasqual.

After a few fraught moments, the nervous, skinny guy spoke.

"I hear birds can't fly this high," he said, his voice shaking a bit.

"I hear only angels can," Mr. Jones replied.

Pasqual nodded. Then he glared challengingly at Mr. Jones, who felt every muscle tense. He was ready, ready for anything. Except for the flight attendant popping up at just the wrong moment.

"Shall I pour your drink?" he asked Mr. Jones, holding a miniature bottle of club soda next to his face as if he were starring in a commercial.

"No," Mr. Jones snapped. "I'll take the bottle. Thank you."

The attendant tried to hand him a glass, but Mr. Jones waved it off. Confused, the attendant headed for that little cubby in the front of the plane where attendants go.

Mr. Jones reached into his dashiki and pulled out a small black velvet pouch. He opened the bag's mouth just enough to show Pasqual the glinting booty inside— diamonds. A fantastic amount of diamonds. Enough diamonds to keep this bony punk in first class indefinitely.

Mr. Jones slipped the bag into Pasqual's trembling hand.

"Here they are," he said. "Now tell me where the bomb is."

"Of course," Pasqual said. A shivery, smarmy grin curled his thin lips. "*I* am the bomb."

Pasqual pulled the lapel of his shabby sport coat away from his chest to reveal a black box strapped beneath one arm. A red detonator signal on the box was blinking away.

I am the bomb? Mr. Jones almost laughed. Talk about melodrama. But he merely shot Pasqual—who was still grinning like an idiot—a stony glare.

Bing.

The cabin went black.

"Wha—" Pasqual blurted. He looked around the plane frantically. Then a small screen buzzed out of the ceiling and flickered on. The in-flight movie had begun.

"Oh. Heh-heh," Pasqual giggled nervously.

Mr. Jones glanced at him impassively. Then he turned his attention to the TV screen.

T. J. Hooker: The Movie, proclaimed the title. The hero, wearing a mustache and packing heat, dashed across the screen.

"Another movie from an old TV show," Mr. Jones snorted, rolling his eyes.

"Well, what're you gonna do?" Pasqual said.

"Walk out," his seatmate replied coolly.

"That's very funny," Pasqual said. The words came out in a squeak.

"No," said Mr. Jones, glaring at Pasqual with the intensity of a hawk. "It isn't."

With a burst of power, Mr. Jones grabbed the emergency door handle and gave it a yank. In three seconds the cabin would decompress, sucking Power-Books, magazines, cocktail peanuts and, perhaps, passengers out into the abyss.

That's why Mr. Jones didn't take that long.

He wrapped Pasqual's neck in a headlock, squeezing with just enough pressure to render him as helpless as an infant, but leaving just enough passage for oxygen. How could he measure such a thing? That's what he'd been trained for.

Then he and Pasqual tumbled backward out of the plane, and the door immediately shut behind them.

The passengers wouldn't have felt more than a light, brief gust of air, Mr. Jones knew. He smiled as he plummeted toward the earth.

Pasqual, however, was not amused.

"Aaaaaahhh," he shrieked. He struggled against Mr. Jones's viselike grip, gazing wildly at the blue abyss below them. They were headed straight into the Pacific Ocean.

"Aaaaaaahh," Pasqual bellowed some more.

Mr. Jones rolled his eyes. Casually, he released one hand from Pasqual, prompting his captive to unleash another round of shrieks, and glanced at his watch. He nodded and gazed across the horizon.

"What's that?" Pasqual yelled, following the man's gaze to a tiny black speck in the distance. The dot zipped toward them, growing larger until it loomed above them, unmistakably a helicopter. It paused. Then a figure launched out of the chopper's open hatch. Headfirst, the skydiver shot sleekly toward them.

Mr. Jones began loosening his grip on Pasqual's chest with his other arm.

"No!" Pasqual screeched, clutching at his captor.

"Pull yourself together," Mr. Jones roared impatiently. "We have company."

Before Pasqual could grunt a reply, the skydiver had hit them and snatched the thief out of Mr. Jones's arms.

Pasqual gaped at the skydiver.

"Y-you're a chick?" he stuttered.

Alex Munday just winked at him. She knew what Pasqual was seeing—your average stunning Asian beauty. Alex had high, honey-colored cheekbones. Her eyes were the color of black coffee and, from what she'd heard, just as seductive. She could also feel her long, shimmering, blue-black locks fluttering out from beneath her helmet.

She hoisted Pasqual under her arm like a rag doll and smirked at Mr. Jones.

"You got bumped?" she quipped over the rushing wind.

"He had too many carry-ons," Mr. Jones retorted, pointing at the still-blinking bomb strapped to Pasqual's chest.

Alex nodded, tightening her grip on her squirming prey. In one deft motion she ripped the bomb off Pasqual and hurled it away. The bomb exploded, sending all three of them flying. But even in midair Alex was a superb navigator. Tumbling head over heels, she still managed to hold on to the terrified and screaming Pasqual. Then she yanked her ripcord.

Whoompf.

Her parachute opened with a roar, pulling them out of their plummet with a violent jerk, still effortlessly maintaining her grip on Pasqual.

Below them, Mr. Jones did a playful flip in the air and then yanked his own ripcord. The cap on his head suddenly became a parachute, shooting skyward in a burst of orange and yellow glory.

October 16, 4:38 P.M.
Location: 19,000 feet above sea level
Wardrobe: Skydiving suit

Now there was nothing to do but float downward. The adrenaline pumping through Alex's blood slowed to a trickle.

"Ho, hum," she said, gazing out at the clouds. Wasn't this always the way, she thought. It's so hard to stay stimulated at the workplace.

After a minute she glanced down. A sleek gold cigarette boat was skimming toward them, hopping whitecaps as if they were cracks in a sidewalk.

"Right on time, Natalie," Alex murmured. The boat positioned itself below them. Alex could see Natalie Cook behind the wheel. Her plump, pink-glossed lips broke into a wide, if slightly shy, smile. Her light blond hair, cut in the very latest in anti-shags, danced above her shoulders, and her blue eyes seemed even brighter next to the sun-dappled water.

Seconds later Alex and her captive dropped neatly onto the deck.

"Nice flight?" Natalie asked coyly.

Alex grinned as she whipped a pair of handcuffs out of her skydiving suit's thigh pocket. She slapped the cuffs on Pasqual's trembling wrists and whipped off her helmet and goggles, shaking out her glossy, stick-straight hair.

Defuse time, Alex thought. My favorite part.

Meanwhile, Natalie turned her attention back to the sky. With casual aplomb, she maneuvered the boat beneath Mr. Jones. In a moment he skimmed onto the deck. He nodded to Alex and Natalie and began gathering up his parachute.

That's when Pasqual lost it. Straining against his cuffs, he spat at Mr. Jones and shrieked, "You crazy son of a——"

"I think you mean daughter," retorted Mr. Jones with a laugh. Then he stepped out of his dashiki. Beneath the billowing robe, he wore a tight black leather skydiving suit. And beneath that suit were some unmistakably female curves. Mr. Jones had the voluptuous bod of any man's dreams.

Pasqual blinked in confusion.

Then Mr. Jones reached beneath his chin and pulled at a flap of skin. Pasqual gasped in horror. With a sickening, tearing sound, Mr. Jones ripped off his own face.

"Aaaaigggh," Pasqual shrieked, throwing his cuffed hands over his eyes.

When he finally peeked, there was Dylan Sanders,

a button-nosed beauty shaking out a shoulder-length mane of auburn waves and tossing a fleshy, latex mask onto the deck.

Mr. Jones was a babe! But she still had the deep, bass voice of a man.

"Come here, baby," she crooned, slithering up to Natalie. Natalie giggled.

"Let's turn out the lights," Dylan sang, swiveling her hips slyly. Then she grinned and rumbled, "Don't need this anymore."

She reached into her mouth and pulled out a silver chip. Then she dropped it casually into a pocket on her skin-tight suit. In her own bewitching voice—part Valley girl, part street-wise Manhattan playa—she announced, "But I could sure use this."

She reached into the dashiki piled at her feet and pulled out the bottle of club soda. Throwing her tousled red hair back, Dylan took a deep swig of the water and poured the rest onto her moisture-deprived face.

As Natalie raced the boat toward shore, Dylan shot Pasqual an icy glare. Then she growled, "Damn, I hate to fly."

THE CHARLES TOWNSEND AGENCY:
Personnel Files

Angel #1: Dylan Sanders

DOB: May 23, 1976
Height: 5´5˝
Hair: Auburn
Eyes: Green
Demeanor: Introspective and brutally independent
Childhood: Mother—deceased; Father—AWOL, possibly deceased. Sanders was a wild child, a rambunctious, rebellious teenager.
Education: Graduated from school with lackluster grades. Did a Kerouac and learned life's lessons on the road.
Employment history: Sanders had a very brief stint at the Police Academy. (See attached report on assault charges filed for punching out a discipline-happy police sergeant.) Since then Sanders has whiled away the days at odd jobs: bartender, yoga instructor, field guide, rodeo entertainer, you name it.
Marital status: Single. Sanders has a knack for choosing jerks, and she's been through a slew of them.
Assets: Always finds the good in people, even jerky guys.
Drawbacks: Where to begin? Sanders is impetuous and has a bad temper. She leaps before she looks. But her determination is superhuman.

Current residence: Bohemian L.A. pad, complete with lava lamps, incense burners, and a less-than-tidy walk-in closet on Melrose Avenue.

Vehicle: Orange-and-white '69 Camaro convertible, license plate number 716-EKL.

Motto: Don't let your past hold you back.

Angel #2: Natalie Cook

DOB: July 13, 1977

Height: 5´9˝

Hair: Platinum blond

Eyes: Pale blue

Demeanor: Somewhat goofy, optimistic, starry-eyed, and shy. Cook is a blusher. She has no idea that she looks like a supermodel and has enough charisma for three. Deceptively brilliant.

Childhood: Mother—large-animal veterinarian; Father—author/editor, most notably of *The Cook Anthology of Science Fiction.* Cook was the class nerd, complete with a Princess Leia honeybun hairdo, glasses, and a mouthful of braces.

Education: Ph.D. from MIT—by correspondence.

Employment history: Research scientist at the Swedish National Academy; U.S. Navy test pilot; Lincoln-Mercury spokesmodel.

Passions: Anything on wheels. Cook is brilliant at road racing, helicopter piloting, and motocross. Trivia. Birding.

Marital Status: Single but ever hopeful.

Drawbacks: Can't dance.

Current residence: Little white bungalow on a canal in Venice, California.
Vehicle: Red Ferrari Modena. License plate number 924-WNP.
Theme song: "Soul Man."

Angel #3: Alex Munday

DOB: September 5, 1975
Height: 5'3"
Hair: Blue-black
Eyes: Dark brown
Demeanor: Sophisticated; a class act; never a hair out of place.
Childhood: Parents: professors of philosophy and economics at Harvard.
Education: By the time she was thirteen, Munday had academically eclipsed her parents. She spent the rest of her teenage years abroad, learning levitation with a Tibetan guru; safecracking and bomb defusing with a Parisian double agent; dancing for a time with the Stuttgart Ballet—the usual classical education. An expert fencer and horsewoman.
Employment history: Government aerospace engineer and on-call consultant for NASA. An early pioneer in the creation of the laptop computer.
Demon: Boredom. Munday is so on top of everything, it's hard to keep her amused.
Marital Status: Single but smitten with Jason Gibbons.

Drawbacks: Nonexistent.
Current residence: An impeccable loft in downtown Los Angeles.
Vehicle: Vintage silver Mercedes convertible, license plate number 340-JAN.
Idol: Martha Stewart.

CHAPTER

1

October 17, 6:42 A.M.
Location: Questionable
Wardrobe: Last night's party togs

Dylan woke up with her head pounding. She opened her eyes slowly. Sunshine! Blinding sunshine! Groaning, Dylan threw her arm over her eyes and burrowed deeper into her pillow. Then she hazily recalled last night's turn of events.

After she and her fellow Angels had delivered Pasqual to the feds, they'd celebrated with a little champagne. She remembered Alex heading home around eleven. Natalie had turned in around one. But Dylan had been up for more partying.

First she'd gone out dancing. Then she'd hit a bar, where she'd challenged every guy in the place to a darts competition. She'd won a hundred bucks in the course of an hour.

Before Dylan could tick off the rest of the evening's adventures, she heard a ghastly warbling. The voice was a man's, but no one would mistake it for one of the Three Tenors.

Dylan blinked and swiped a hand over her eyes. Then she blinked again.

This faux-wood-paneled, shag-carpeted houseboat with the frayed curtains, leopard-print sheets, and that funky eau-de-bachelor scent (a melange of sweat socks, grilled cheese sandwiches, and cheap hair gel) was not her cool Melrose Avenue pad. It was the full-time abode of her on-again, off-again boyfriend, Chad. Currently they were in one of their off modes.

"Oh, no," Dylan moaned, heaving herself to the edge of the bed and fumbling for her white tank top and jeans. As she shimmied into them, a googly-eyed dude appeared in the doorway—Chad. He was all fuzzy goatee and jutting Adam's apple, and he held a frying pan filled with sizzling scrambled eggs.

"Morning, starfish," Chad said, leering goofily at Dylan.

Dylan closed her eyes, and the last bit of the evening came rushing back to her. That's right—after dancing the night away, she'd felt too tired to drive her own vintage Camaro home. So, certain of a welcome, she'd decided to spend the night at Chad's.

And now here he was, in long red underwear and big rubber boots, wielding toxic-smelling breakfast food. Dylan felt her stomach lurch, but she smiled wanly and said, "Morning, Chad."

Chad waved the frying pan in Dylan's direction and winked.

"So," he said, "I figured we could have a little breakfast and then maybe have a little Chad."

Oh, God. He thinks we're on again, Dylan

thought, but she was distracted by a high-pitched *bleep, bleep*.

Saved by the cell phone.

"Hold that thought," Dylan said to Chad. Then she flopped back on the bed, dug into her Levi's back pocket for the phone and flipped it open.

"Yeah?" she said. The familiar voice on the other end made her sit up. "Okay. Right. I'll be right there."

Dylan clicked the phone shut and turned to face Chad. She planted an oh-so-fake disappointed frown on her face and said, "Isn't that just the luck." Then she sprang off the bed, pulled on her boots, and hurried to the ladder that would take her away from this dark and dank bachelor pad. She scurried up the steps.

"We'd better be docked," she muttered. She squinted in the harsh sunshine and saw that the boat was moored at a marina on the wrong side of the tracks in Santa Monica. Yes! She shoved her cell phone into her pocket and began to climb down a ladder onto the dock.

Chad followed her and stood on deck. He was still clutching the pan of eggs, and his weak chin was practically wobbling with disappointment.

"I could make something else if you don't like eggs," he offered.

Dylan jumped off the boat, landing on the dock.

"It's not the eggs," she tossed over her shoulder as she stalked down the dock.

"Is it the boat?" Chad called, waving his frying pan helplessly.

Dylan stopped and sighed. She gazed at Chad and planted her fists on her hips.

"No, it's not the boat," she insisted. "Look, I have to go."

"Is it the Chad?" he asked her feebly.

"It might be the Chad," Dylan blurted, and then she bit her lip. There was something sort of sweet about Chad, standing there all skinny and pathetic with those stupid scrambled eggs.

Dylan reached deep into her kindness reserve and blew Chad a kiss, then gave him a sweet smile. She watched the projected response flash across Chad's face—surprise, delight, hope—and then she turned on her heel and hurried away.

Dylan focused all her energy on the pavement. I am walking away, she thought. I will get into my car and head directly to the agency without stopping at Go. Or anywhere else.

She sighed as she turned the key in the Camaro's ignition. Then she muttered, "What a way to start my vacation."

October 17, 6:51 A.M.
Location: A trailer on the set of _L.A. Underwater_,
    Pacific Pictures studio lot
Quandary: Blueberry, chocolate chip, or lemon poppy
    seed?

Mmmm, what a way to start my vacation, Alex thought happily. She paused as she stirred a bowlful of muffin batter and dipped her finger into the lumpy liquid. Putting her fingertip into her mouth, she tasted flour and an overwhelming amount of salt.

Oh no, she thought. Is salt bad? I followed the recipe! The salt must, like, evaporate in the oven or something.

Alex sighed and glanced at her last batch of muffins, or rather, blackened, withered attempts-at-muffins. She just didn't get it. She had designed the hyperjet thruster engine for the space shuttle; she could crack any safe and translate any covert code; she could kickbox any thug into oblivion. But this cooking thing? It was kicking her butt.

Especially while she was simultaneously running lines with her movie actor sweetie, Jason Gibbons. He had a multifilm contract and the deepest dimples known to womankind.

He also had a funky vintage Airstream trailer with a stocked minibar and full kitchen.

Now, if only he had my photographic memory, Jason would be perfect, Alex thought, glancing at the script in Jason's hand. Jason had a dazzling toothy grin and pecs that just wouldn't quit, but when it came to acting . . . Well, Alex thought loyally, who really wants great acting from their movie stars these days?

She shot Jason an affectionate smile. He gazed back at her with gooey adoration.

Then he put on his "intense" face and squared his shoulders in his macho costume—a tight black T-shirt and fake scar—and read from his script:

"If you don't defuse this bomb, Logan," he growled, "L.A.'s going to be a new underwater attraction."

Then he reverted to his own sweet, slightly confused self and said to Alex, "This is so stupid. Why wouldn't I just yank the wires?"

"No, honey," she said absently, slipping on an oven mitt. "You see, those are dummy wires. The real mechanism is inside and is encased in a titanium shell. If you trip the external feedback circuit, the bomb will detonate."

Then Alex glared back at her recipe. "Baking soda, baking powder. What's the difference." She was scowling and stared at her gruel-like muffin batter when she noticed Jason looking at her funny.

"Wow," he said. "For a bikini waxer, you know a lot about bombs."

Oops.

"Uh, isn't it amazing," Alex stuttered, "what you can pick up on the Internet?"

Jason giggled and cupped Alex's face in his hands. He was leaning in, lips puckered . . .

Bleep-bleep.

"Aw," Jason said. Alex sighed. Smooch abandoned, they both reached for their cell phones on the kitchen counter.

"Mine," Alex said, scooping up her phone with her oven mitt and flipping it open. "Hello?"

She frowned as she listened to the message squawking through her cell.

"Okay. I'll be right there," she said. Then she

clicked her phone shut and headed for the trailer door.

"Awww." Jason pouted some more. "Can't you call in sick?"

"I can't," Alex said briskly, straightening her strapless leather corset, grabbing her muffin basket and opening the door. "It's an emergency."

Before Jason could call her bluff, a nervous, clipboard-carrying production assistant type sidled up to the trailer.

"They're ready for you on the set, Mr. Gibbons," he said.

"Yeah," Jason said. Then he turned back to Alex and laid one cinematic smooch on her lips. When he came up for air he shot Alex his matinee-idol, lopsided grin.

"Gotta go save the world," he said.

"My hero," Alex flirted back. She winked at him as she broke off a piece of poppy-seed muffin. Then she batted her eyelashes and popped the morsel into Jason's mouth.

"Oof!" Jason grunted. "I mean, mmmmm." He struggled to smile and his eyes watered.

He must really love lemon poppy seed, Alex thought happily. I'll have to make more. Then she turned on her heel and headed to her silver Mercedes convertible, which she'd parked right next to Jason's trailer on the studio lot. She turned to wave goodbye.

"When do I get to meet this Charlie?" Jason called, flashing a nervous smile.

"Charlie's not very social," Alex replied.

"But it's a chick, right?" he said, cocking his head hopefully. "Charlie's a woman?"

Alex gazed at Jason. Jealousy? Ah, actors—so sweet, so simple. Alex couldn't help but play with her boy-toy a little. So she merely winked and opened her car door. As she settled into the seat, Jason shook his head and gazed at her with a look that was half frustration, half awe.

Then Alex gunned her motor and shifted into gear. She was outta there.

October 17, the wee hours
Location: Disco Inferno, the hottest club on Sunset Strip
Status: Belle of the ball

Natalie stalked up to the doorway of the Inferno. Velvet rope, shmelvet rope. She never had any trouble getting into the club. After all, when Natalie wore her lucky outfit—a slinky pale blue number encrusted with tiny crystals—the dancing world bowed at her feet.

Besides, she was a regular.

She sashayed into the club, watching the eyes of every man, woman, and . . . man swivel toward her.

"Hey, Natalie," shouted a crowd of cool guys by the bar. Natalie smiled at them and bobbed her head to the throbbing dance music. She gave each groovy fella a high-five as she shimmied past.

"Natalie, you made it!" cried another admirer. Natalie winked at him. Then she bellied up to the bar. The bartender dropped what he was doing and ran to help his most babe-alicious customer.

"Your usual, Natalie?" he chirped.

"Not shaken, not stirred," she cooed.

In an instant, Natalie was sipping a frothy, mango Mai-Tai-ish concoction. She paid the bartender with a killer smile.

"Gee, thanks!" he cried.

"Right on," she said, before she strutted over to the dance floor. Behind her trailed the cream of Disco Inferno's male crop—hipsters in black, millionaires in diamond studs, trust-funders in Gucci.

But Natalie had eyes only for the DJ, a suave and slender fellow spinning tunage from behind a mixing board.

"Eduardo," Natalie ordered. "Move me!"

Eduardo shot Natalie a thumbs-up and launched a devastating Latin beat into the air.

Salsa!

Natalie's hips began to swivel, and her feet began to shimmy. She spun into the arms of one man, luring him into a tango dip. Before he could embrace her, she shimmied to another dude, rocking her hips against his.

Then Eduardo segued into disco. Without missing a beat, Natalie was doing her best *Saturday Night Fever* shag, leading an adoring gaggle of partiers in a group groove.

Then it was a *Flashdance* riff. Natalie was in the middle of a dramatic head-whirl when she heard the

bartender announce, "It's Natalie's world"—*beep*—
"we just"—*beep*—"live in it."

Beep. Beep. Beep.

October 17, 6:59 A.M.
Location: Natalie Cook's bedroom
Reality check: Wakey, wakey

Natalie's eyes popped open, and Eduardo, her bartender admirer, her frothy Mai Tai—all of her glory—
poofed away.

But Natalie was still wearing her grin. She leaped
out of bed, directly into her left slipper. Then she
popped her other foot into her right slipper.

Still shimmying to the disco inferno in her head,
Natalie swiveled her hips in her Spider-Man Underoos
and began making her bed.

"What a *feel*-ing," she sang as she yanked drum-
tight hospital corners into place. She grabbed a quar-
ter from her nightstand and bounced it off the bed.

Perfect.

Natalie was shimmying past her alphabetized
record album stacks and her troll doll collection to the
bathroom, when her morning routine was interrupted
by the doorbell.

"Who could that be?" Natalie blurted, tossing on a
baby-doll robe and heading for the door.

"UPS!" said a man in brown shorts. His eyes
bulged admiringly when Natalie stepped into the
doorway, pushing her disheveled blond locks out of

her eyes and feeling the sun splash onto her long, tanned legs.

"I hope you don't mind my coming so early," the delivery dude said, handing Natalie an electronic pad to sign.

"You know, I signed the release waiver thing," Natalie murmured as she autographed the virtual notepad. "So you don't have to ring the doorbell. Just feel free to stick things in the slot."

"Uh-huh," the UPS guy replied, his eyes bulging just a tad wider. Not that Natalie noticed or anything. She was transfixed by the UPS truck, pinging and knocking and huffing in the driveway.

"I'd recommend springing for the premium diesel," she said, grabbing the package out of UPS-boy's hands. "Treat the old girl right and she'll run like a dream forever."

The delivery man looked rapturous. In fact, he looked a little faint. Natalie had no idea. She knocked the door closed with her hip and peered at her package.

"My animé classics library!" she cried, whipping a Japanese videotape from the envelope. "Excellent!"

Bleeeeep.

Natalie bopped over to the phone and answered on the first ring.

"Hello," she sang. She stopped shimmying when she heard the voice on the other line and went all business. "I'll be right in."

And in 16.4 carefully calibrated minutes, Natalie was decked out in cigarette pants, a shiny, wine-colored blouse and her favorite blue Manolos. She gathered up her munchies, locked the front door, hopped into her fly red Ferrari Modena, and gunned it for Beverly Hills.

It was Natalie's world. Everybody else just lived in it.

CHAPTER

2

October 17, 8:48 A.M.
Location: Charles Townsend Detective Agency, Beverly Hills
Trial: Breakfast by Alex

Dylan stood at the bar in the Charles Townsend Agency—the girl detectives' home away from home—pouring herself a California cappuccino. (That would be iced tea.)

She took a long slurp from her glass and flopped onto one of the sleek, modern, cream-colored couches. She felt better now that she'd gone home and changed into a black suit and a pretty champagne-colored chemise.

The agency—all pale green walls, mod bar stools, hardwood floors and subtle artwork—always made her feel better, too. She knew Alex and Natalie felt much the same way, though it was something they'd never really discussed.

Most of all, Dylan found comfort in the retro cream-colored box on the desk. It was through this box that Dylan, Natalie, Alex, and Bosley—their office manager, tech support guy, and surrogate favorite uncle—heard from their boss.

Charlie, Dylan thought, our elusive head honcho. Charlie was the man who'd brought Dylan, Alex, and Natalie together. He was the one who'd dubbed them Angels. He'd rescued them from their boring day jobs.

Natalie, a five-time *Jeopardy* champion, had been at the Swedish National Academy chemistry lab, where discovering one vaccine after another was just . . . getting old.

And Alex had been languishing in the ivory tower of academia where, sure, she was one of the most sought-after lecturers on the aerospace circuit. And yes, she did a little work for NASA on the side. But where was the *challenge?*

And Dylan? Well, after a *very* brief stint at the police academy, Dylan had just been bumming around, playing too hard, getting one tattoo after another, and waiting for the perfect opportunity.

Before they'd become Charlie's Angels, they'd spoken a dozen languages between them. They could hack themselves into any computer system. They could bench-press three-hundred pounds.

But Charlie had added those little extras that made all the difference: kung fu instruction from the foremost authority in Hong Kong; classified technology in bugging and tracking devices; and, most important, really cool cars and an astronomical wardrobe budget.

The only thing Charlie didn't give them, Dylan thought ruefully, was his presence.

They had never met Charlie in person. He was just a gravelly, charismatic voice on a speakerphone at the Charles Townsend Detective Agency—an international man of mystery without the British accent.

Dylan sighed and glanced at her fellow Angels. Natalie was sprawled on the other couch, idly resting her stiletto-heeled feet on the arm and flipping through a book on bird calls.

Alex came over to the coffee table, planted her basket of muffins down with a thunk and put her hands on her hips.

"You guys," she announced, "I don't think I can keep up the facade with Jason anymore."

Dylan sat up. Alex looked serious. "Well, you can't tell him the truth," Dylan said to her bud.

"Just tell him you love him," Natalie suggested dreamily. "Love conquers all."

Alex rolled her eyes.

"Look, it's a fact," she said. "Some men are intimidated by a strong woman—"

"Who holds a seventh degree black belt," Dylan pointed out.

"And can hack through the Pentagon's firewall," Natalie piped up.

"Yeah," Alex said with a pout. "They come on all lovey-dovey until they find out I can shatter a cinderblock with my forehead."

She sighed.

But Alex was a sensible genius. Brooding was counterproductive. So, after thirty seconds in a funk, she perked up. She grabbed her muffin basket and thrust it toward Dylan and Natalie.

"Blueberry muffins?" she said. "Made 'em from scratch!"

Uh-oh, Dylan thought. Muffins by Alex? Or should I say Death by Concrete? She shot Natalie a baleful look. Natalie was white and wide-eyed. She was trying to smile. She reached for a muffin with a trembling hand. Dylan grabbed one, too.

Thank goodness for that torture-resistance training Charlie sent us to in Thailand, Dylan thought. Then she lifted the muffin to her lips.

Ack. ACK! Dylan was dying inside. Clearly, Natalie was in the same fix.

"Yummmm," the blond Angel choked, trying to smile at Alex. Alex grinned. Then she turned to Dylan.

"Oh-oh," Dylan stammered, trying to swallow the bit of salty sawdust in her mouth. Alex smiled again. She went to put a muffin on Bosley's desk.

As soon as Alex turned her back, Dylan let her face crumple with disgust.

"Mayday," she whispered, whipping her muffin at Natalie. Natalie dodged the crumbly missile with a giggle.

"SOS!" she hissed back. She winged her own pastry at Dylan's head, but Dylan dove out of the way. The muffin hit the agency's front door with a loud crack, just as Bosley, their hapless henchman, was walking in.

Bosley—a man with a mysterious past and even

more mysterious present—was a portrait of aging Hollywood in all its glory. He was dressed impeccably in black pants, black mock-turtleneck, and snazzy sports coat. But there was no disguising his tired old bod. He had the pallor and gray eye-bags of a man who'd spent many an hour in L.A. traffic. He had a slight paunch. He had fuzzy, thinning gray hair that had an uncommon way of never staying put.

And of course, he was an endless source of wry wit.

"What do you call these?" he asked the Angels, regarding the rock-hard muffin imbedded in the now-splintered agency door.

"Chinese fighting muffins," Dylan said. Her pouty red lips twitched as she tried to suppress a smile. Natalie just had to giggle again.

Bosley eyed the Angels seriously.

"Nothin' to laugh about," he intoned. "Buddy of mine took a fighting muffin to the chest. Sent him home in four Ziploc bags."

Alex, who'd been positioning Bosley's muffin on a doily, just so, whirled around and glared at her colleagues.

"They're not Chinese, and they're not fighting," she yelled. "They're blueberry."

Then she flung herself on the couch next to Natalie. Dylan moved to sit next to her and patted her knee.

"You okay, Alex?" Bosley said carefully.

"She's having trouble with her secret identity," Natalie said.

"Aren't we all." Bosley sighed, crossing the room. "Scooch."

The Angels wriggled out of the way, and Bosley sat on the couch between them, taking Alex's hand in his.

"Alex," Bosley said, looking into her eyes. "All my Angels. The heart . . . is a muscle. In body-building, we exercise the muscle until it tears, and when that tear heals, the muscle is bigger and stronger. And it's the same with the heart."

"I must have the heart of a rhino," Dylan blurted.

"You do," Bosley said, squeezing Dylan's arm. "And you be proud of it. *Mes anges,* the little hurts will heal. And at crunch time, your hearts will be so buff, you'll be able to clean and jerk his love three sets, ten reps each."

"Thanks, Bos," Natalie chirped.

"*Merci,* Bosley," Alex said quietly.

"Thank you, Bosley," Dylan said, giving him a playful punch in the bicep. Bosley winced and gave a little yelp, just as the clock hit 9 A.M. and the phone began ringing.

"I'll get that," Bosley grunted.

Dylan tensed—that would be Charlie on the phone. He called Bosley every morning at nine on the dot. Even so, Dylan couldn't help feeling a little charge every time their mysterious bossman called with a new challenge.

The speakerphone came alive. It broadcast a strong, soothing voice—a little gravelly, a little sharp, but somehow just right.

"Good morning, Angels," said the voice.

"Good morning, Charlie," the Angels replied in a teasing singsong.

"Alex, Dylan, Natalie, we've got a case that just can't wait," Charlie said.

As Charlie spoke, a sleek, up-to-the-minute plasma screen video monitor descended from the ceiling. The automatic Venetian blinds hummed shut, blocking out the bright morning sun.

The monitor flickered on, and the screen filled with the image of a dashing young guy. He had straight, dark hair that flopped over his brooding eyes. Even on a video monitor you could see they were a dark, cocoa brown. His face was just imperfect enough to be ruggedly handsome.

At the bottom of the screen a caption read, "Next on *Night Time Live,* Rags to Riches—tech whiz's company built from the ground up."

And indeed, this guy looked every bit the dot-com millionaire in baggy khakis and running shoes and wire-rimmed glasses. One shot showed him at a black-tie gala, yanking at the collar of his tux uncomfortably. In another he was piloting a slick black two-seater helicopter.

"Meet Eric Knox," Charlie said. "He's a brilliant engineer and the founder of a promising young communications software company."

"Uh-huh," Natalie said.

"Last night," Charlie continued, "Knox was kidnapped while attending a charity ball downtown."

As Charlie spoke, the video monitor flashed from crisp, color footage to the grainy black-and-white of a surveillance camera. The setting was clearly a dingy parking garage. And there was Eric Knox, strolling toward his BMW with a stunning, tall woman in a mink wrap and a neat, brunette chignon.

Suddenly two beefy men in black caps leaped out from behind a dark-colored sedan. They lunged at Knox, shoving the woman aside. She lost her balance and fell to her knees.

The thugs pinned Knox's arms behind his back and hoisted him into the backseat of the sedan. The car darted out of camera range, leaving two angry skid marks on the cement. The beautiful woman lurched to her feet. With that, the image froze.

"Who's the supermodel?" Alex asked.

"Mr. Knox's partner and co-chairman of his company," Charlie answered.

Natalie pointed at the screen.

"She did it," she announced.

A voice—a female voice—filled the room.

"Then I guess we can all go home."

The angels turned toward the office door. There stood the woman they'd just seen on Eric Knox's kidnapping video. She wore an impeccable, buttonless gray suit, $500 lizard heels, and the kind of refined bone structure you can't buy, not even in L.A. She seemed fully recovered from the previous night's trauma.

"Angels," Bosley said, getting to his feet. "Meet Vivian Wood, our new client. She's hired us to find Mr. Knox."

Dylan shot Natalie a sympathetic look. Busted.

Natalie was squirming and avoiding Vivian Wood's eyes. Dylan would bail her out. She cleared her throat and went all professional.

"Ms. Wood," Dylan said, "who would have the most to gain from Knox's disappearance?"

"Me, probably," the woman said, stalking across the room and placing her buttery leather purse on Bosley's desk, next to the speakerphone. She perched on the edge of the desk, shot Natalie an icy glare, and then regarded Dylan again. "I'm his partner. But long before we were partners we were friends."

"Does Knox have any enemies to speak of?" Natalie asked.

Charlie cut in.

"Roger Corwin," he said.

The video monitor sprang to life again. This time the screen was filled with a scary close-up of a beady-eyed man. He was your average sleaze, with teeth that were too perfectly white, a deep tan, and a goatee. He seemed to have a facial expression repertoire of two: a menacing scowl and an attempt at a smile that looked more like a painful leer.

Alex gazed at Corwin's face and nodded knowingly.

"Corwin's the owner of Red Star Systems," she explained. "It's the biggest telecommunications satellite firm in the world."

A photo appeared on the screen—Corwin in a black silk kimono, standing smugly before his Japanese art collection. Next an image of *Hostile Takeover Monthly* magazine popped up. Corwin was on the cover, red-faced and screaming. The headline read, "Destroying the Competition."

Then there was a shaky, hand-held shot of Corwin unfurling his tall barrel-chested self out of a limo. On his arm was a bleached-blond chippie.

"Where'd he find her," Dylan asked. "Rent a date?"

Finally, Corwin's logo, a red star in a circle, filled the screen. The lights went up. Bosley pulled a stack of dossiers from his briefcase and handed one to each Angel.

"Six months ago," Vivian explained, "Corwin tried to buy out Knox Technologies. When Knox wouldn't sell, Corwin just lost it."

Bosley shook his head and sighed sadly.

"Charming," he said. "He can't buy out Knox, so he hits him over the head and throws him in the back of a car."

Vivian emitted a little gasp. Bosley whirled around to see her pressing a handkerchief to her mouth.

"Oh, jeez," Bosley said gently, "I'm sorry. But how can we be sure that Knox is still alive?"

"Has there been any ransom demand?" Alex asked Vivian.

"Or any word at all from Knox or the kidnappers?" Natalie chimed in.

Vivian shook away the tears that were pooling in her eyes and squared her shoulders.

"Nothing," she said. "But I know he's alive. I just know it."

The Angels looked at Vivian sympathetically.

Clearly, this babe was harboring a major yen for her "partner." Natalie forgot about the eat-dirt glare Vivian had given her not long ago. She went to the woman's side.

"I'll study the video footage and see what I can come up with," she offered.

"So Corwin is your best and only lead," Alex said. "Hopefully, he'll take us to Knox." She leaped to her feet. Alex always got a rush from a new case—she was raring to go.

The three Angels looked at the speakerphone, awaiting marching orders from their boss.

"Every Monday, Corwin gets a massage at Madame Wong's House of Blossoms," Charlie said. "That's your chance for a little . . . undercover work."

The Angels smirked and glanced at one another.

"Be careful, Angels," Charlie added. "Corwin plays rough."

Dylan looked coyly at the speakerphone as if it were the man himself. She had come to regard the box as an almost live thing. If she stared hard enough at the round, speckled speaker, she could see her vision of Charlie's face there. She imagined he had brown eyes and smoothed-back, red-tinged hair. He had laugh lines around his eyes and a sun-kissed, life-is-good glow in his skin.

"Sounds like we could use you, Charlie?" she asked.

"I'd love to, Angels, but I've got my hands full this morning," the speaker answered. Dylan cocked her head—what was that sound swirling around Charlie's voice. If she didn't know better, she'd swear it was the whistle of high-altitude wind shear. The kind you heard on the face of a mountain.

Before Dylan had a chance to wonder just *where* their big cheese was calling from, Charlie spoke again.

"Good luck, Angels," he said in farewell.

Then with a little click, the phone went silent.

Charlie's departure left the Angels, Bosley, and Vivian Wood with a pocket of dead air among them. There was nothing to do but dive into their mission headfirst.

CHAPTER

3

October 17, 1:34 P.M.
Location: Madame Wong's House of Blossoms, a
    Sino-Japanese spa. Massage room
Wardrobe: Strategic sheeting

Roger Corwin was lying facedown on a massage
table in one of Madame Wong's poshest private
rooms. He was primed for his massage, a sheet draped
around his midsection. The only thing he wore was a
key hanging from a leather cord around his wrist. And
relaxation? Forget about it—the satellite magnate
was yammering into a cell phone.

"He said what? Over his dead body?" Corwin
barked into the cell. "I can accept those terms."

He snickered and slammed his phone shut. Then
he twisted around and cast a baleful glance at the
masseuse, who had her back to him.

"If you don't mind, I'd like to get started this mil-
lennium," he huffed.

Alex planted a submissive smile on her lips and
turned toward Corwin, feeling her silky kimono graz-
ing her thighs. She tried to move her head as little as

possible, so as not to unbalance her heavy, itchy Geisha-girl wig.

"Of course," she murmured, approaching Corwin's back. Uch, she thought, ever hear of sunscreen? He's as leathery as an old shoe.

Using a low stepstool, Alex climbed onto the table and began to walk on Corwin's back, massaging each vertebra as she went.

"Ooof," Corwin grunted as Alex's powerful toes found the pressure points in his shoulders. "Oooooh, that's good, honey."

"You're carrying a lot of tension along the fourth and fifth vertebrae," Alex commented. "Let me see if I can work it out."

She kneaded Corwin's back, holding onto a rod in the ceiling for balance. Then she proceeded to the base of his neck.

"Urghhhh," Corwin sighed. "You're a genius."

Alex rolled her eyes. Yuck. She bent down and pulled Corwin's arms away from his sides.

"The human body is an amazing instrument," she said, wedging her big toe into the base of Corwin's neck. She continued to speak soothingly.

"Just by activating the right energy points, you can improve circulation, alleviate pain or . . ."

Alex felt Corwin's knotty shoulders go limp.

". . . knock a man unconscious."

Alex bent down and peered into Corwin's face. He was out like last year's hip-huggers. She slid the cord from Corwin's wrist and glanced at his key. Locker #509.

Silently Alex opened the massage room door for Dylan and Natalie, also wearing wigs and kimonos. Alex gave a little bird whistle, then tossed Dylan the key, gave her a wink, and clicked the door shut behind her.

October 17, 1:46 P.M.
Location: Madame Wong's House of Blossoms. Executive locker room
Status: A little breaking and entering in the afternoon

All three Angels quickly made their way to the executive locker room and stole inside. An efficient once-over assured them they were alone. They found Corwin's locker and clicked the key into place.

Dylan stood guard while Alex began to riffle through Corwin's things.

"Let's see," Alex muttered. "Mini-shampoos stolen from hotel bathrooms, a *Sports Illustrated* swimsuit issue, a napkin with someone's phone number on it. Oh, and what have we here?"

She pulled a handgun out of Corwin's gym bag and showed it to Natalie.

"Classy guy," Natalie said with a sneer.

Next Alex came across Corwin's Palm Pilot. Pulling a small holster from the sash of her kimono, she plugged the Pilot into it. The device whirred and bleeped softly as it downloaded every bit of information in the tiny computer.

Then Natalie discovered Corwin's car keys. She pulled out a powder compact, or rather a small dish of soft clay disguised as a powder compact. She took the Bentley key and pressed it into the clay mold, making an instant impression.

Finito. Natalie swiftly replaced everything and closed the locker. Then the Angels breezed out of the room and raced stealthily back to the massage room.

October 17, 1:55 P.M.
Location: Madame Wong's House of Blossoms,
    massage room
Mission: Accomplished

Corwin snorted and opened his eyes. He felt dizzy and the room looked hazy. He craned his neck and peered over his shoulder.

There was his pretty Geisha girl, massaging away.

Then he looked at his wrist. There was his locker key, right where he'd left it.

"You must have dozed off," Alex crooned.

Corwin blinked heavily.

"You're very good with your hands," he muttered. "I could use someone like you on my staff."

"Thanks for the offer," Alex said, sneering at Corwin's back. "But my hands aren't going anywhere near your staff.

"And guess what?" she added, letting just the tiniest bit of venom enter her voice. "Time's up."

October 17, 3:50 P.M.
Location: Tastee Freeze, the drive-through queue
Task: Downloading and downtime

Alex, Natalie, and Dylan had ditched their wigs and tossed on comfy halter tops, jean jackets, and wedgies. Then they'd jumped into Dylan's orange-and-white hot rod and gone on a junk-food run.

As Dylan pulled up to the drive-through window, Alex gaped at a flower-strewn magazine in her lap.

"That Martha Stewart is amazing!" she exclaimed, turning to Dylan. Natalie was huddled in the back-seat with a portable video monitor, inspecting Knox's kidnapping tape in super-slo-mo.

"Martha can take old grocery bags," Alex enthused, "and turn them into gorgeous nondenominational holiday wrapping paper."

Dylan stared at Alex for a moment. She cocked an eyebrow at her Betty Crocker-wannabe bud.

"Yeah," Dylan finally said. "But can she kick five guys' butts while saving hostages from a burning building?"

Alex gave Dylan a playful karate chop to the solar plexus while Dylan drove up to the drive-through menu.

"Czmea tok yosh odinguh," squawked the intercom.

Alex jerked her eyes away from a feature on creating your own spackle from egg whites and toothpaste.

"Czmea tok yosh odinguh, przh," squawked the box.

Alex huffed irritably. Incompetence was everywhere! She grabbed the Swiss Army knife hanging from Dylan's rearview mirror. (Dylan just wasn't a fuzzy dice kind of girl.)

"Just a minute," Alex shouted at the drive-through speaker. Then she flopped over Dylan's lap and reached for the speaker. Flipping open the box's lid, she used the knife to fish out a couple of wires. She futzed with them for ten seconds and slammed the box shut.

"May I take your order, please," said a crystal-clear voice in the box.

Dylan grinned at her tech-genius co-Angel and said, "Three double-doubles, three fries, three Cokes."

As she headed to the pick-up window, Dylan heard a whirring in the backseat. Natalie's built-in video printer had just spit out a color image. She handed it to her buds in the front seat.

"I found a clean frame on one of the kidnappers," she said.

"And looks like we've got all of Corwin's Palm Pilot data transferred, too," Alex said, looking at the blinking hub on the seat next to her. Her own Palm Pilot had been uploading the information snitched from Corwin's computer.

Alex took the photo from Natalie and shared a peek with Dylan.

Everything about the kidnapper was long and skinny. He had a pointy nose, beady eyes, wispy, slick black hair and a grim, lipless mouth. He was pale to the point of disappearing, and his eyes were icy blue. He was sinister as all get-out.

"We have a bad guy in the Thin Man here," Dylan mused. "Now all we have to do is look for him."

"And see if he's working for Corwin," Natalie said. She hung over the back of the front seat and glared at the picture.

"Well, what do you know," Alex said. "There's a prerace shindig for the Dash for Cash at Corwin's apartment in Chinatown tonight."

Then she feasted her buds with a let's-get-ready-to-rumble grin.

"Who's up for a party?"

October 17, 8:46 P.M.
Location: A Chinatown street near Roger Corwin's
    apartment building
Wardrobe: Smart choppers

The Angels, including Bosley, sat in Bos's Stutz Blackhawk, gazing up at the party pad—the penthouse of a glimmering glass-and-steel skyscraper planted arrogantly in the heart of Chinatown.

The Angels' faces were clenched with determination and moxie—their usual premission state. Bosley was trembling like a baby. Dylan graciously did her best to ignore his quaking as she reached into the cleavage of her black velvet gown and pulled out transparent tooth-shaped caps with tiny silver chips in them.

She passed one to each Angel. Natalie showed hers to Bosley.

"Okay," she explained, "this is a mic/transmitter. It's like a cap. Just snap it on over a rear molar . . ."

Bosley popped the mic into his mouth and slipped it over his tooth.

"I know," he said nervously. "A mouth mic. I know."

Alex slipped her mic on and placed a minuscule radio receiver into her ear. Bosley, Natalie, and Dylan put their receivers into place as well.

"We'll be able to stay in contact the whole time," Alex said, squeezing Bos's shoulder.

Then the Angels thrust their hands together, palm atop palm—a grip of solidarity. This was their premission ritual. They never forgot it.

But this time an additional, slightly hairier hand would be in on the mix.

"Get in here, Bos," Dylan ordered with a grin.

Bosley stopped trembling and smiled at his girls. He slapped his hand on top of theirs.

"Angels forever," the quartet chanted.

CHAPTER

4

October 17, 9:01 P.M.
Location: Roger Corwin's penthouse bachelor pad
Status: Deep cover

Dylan almost gasped as the elevator doors opened onto Roger Corwin's rooftop garden.

Wow, she thought, gazing at the Koi-populated stream, the teak bridges and walkways, the cherry trees in full, off-season bloom. Corwin must have paid millions for this status pad.

Bosley tossed one arm around Dylan's waist and the other around Alex. He sauntered up to a beefy guy on security duty near the elevator. In fact, Dylan noticed, thuggish-looking men with walkie-talkies were stationed all around the garden.

Bosley lowered his tinted aviator glasses and spoke with false pomposity.

"John David Rage," he announced to the guard. He leered suggestively at the Angels on his arms and added, "Plus two." Then he winked at the guard and gave him a thumbs-up.

Dylan just had to let loose a laugh. She stifled it

quickly and blew Bosley a kiss while the security dude checked them out: Alex in a jewel-studded red sheath with a flowing train; Dylan in an off-the-shoulder, black slinky number. Bosley, meanwhile, looked . . . dashing? He wore a satin paisley smoking jacket and a high-collared, yellow shirt with a garish tie pin.

The security thug yawned and waved them in. Bosley leaned down and whispered to the Angels, "We're in deep cover now, so if you forget *John David,* call me J. D., like—"

"Jelly Doughnut," Alex provided, grinning.

"Jack Daniels," Dylan said.

"Juvenile Delinquent?" Alex giggled.

Bosley ignored the girls' ribbing and kept up his *Mission: Impossible* thing.

"Okay," he whispered. "Whoever runs into Corwin first, keeps him busy."

"Right," Alex agreed.

"Let's go to work," Dylan said, giving Bosley's pillowy waist a little squeeze. Then Alex and Dylan slipped away into a crowd of tuxedoed players, society babes, model/actresses, and cocktail waitresses in baby-doll kimonos.

Bosley was standing awkwardly in the middle of a terrace, trying to blend, when someone tapped him on the shoulder. Bosley turned and stifled a squeak.

"Roger Corwin," said the someone, giving Bosley a wide, welcoming grin through his goatee. He thrust his hand out for a hearty shake. Two voluptuous trophy dates with vacant eyes trailed behind Corwin, looking bored.

"Welcome," the sinister host said to Bosley.

"John David Rage," Bosley introduced himself. "Self-help guru."

Corwin looked puzzled.

"John David *Rage?*" he questioned.

Oh, no! Bosley thought. My pseudonym is too macho, isn't it? I've threatened Corwin with my machoness. Have I blown it?

"I am *thirsty,*" Bosley announced nervously. He pointed to Corwin and his girlfriends. "Hammerhead? Hammerhead?"

Then he tapped a comely blond in standard cater-waiter gear on the shoulder.

"Excuse me, miss," he said.

The waitress turned around and blinked at Bosley with crystal blue eyes just like Natalie's. Natalie!

"Oh!" Bosley cried, recognizing her. He cleared his throat and recovered quickly.

"A round of Hammerheads, please, miss," he ordered.

"Sure," Natalie chirped. She winked at Bos and headed to the bar.

Bosley turned back to Corwin to find the leather-faced man scrutinizing Bosley's garish getup.

"I admire your taste, Mr. Rage," he said. Then he raised one eyebrow and added, "If that *is* indeed your name."

"Back at you, R. C.," Bosley replied. He flipped around so Corwin couldn't see the panic in his eyes. "This place, it's Japanese, is it not?"

"Good eye, J. D.," Corwin said. He was staring at

Bosley's upper lip, which was beaded with nervous sweat. Bosley covered his mouth, trying to subtly flick the moisture away.

The molar mic! Bosley ripped his hand away from his mouth as he suddenly remembered his toothy, bugging device. He had to be on the ball. He, Boy Angel Bosley, had cornered Corwin, and it was up to him to record every word the man said.

Bosley leaned close to Corwin and opened his mouth slightly, trying not to let his tongue hang out.

Corwin looked askance at him and raised one eyebrow. But he continued showing off his palatial digs.

"It's a thirteenth-century Shinto temple. Priceless," he explained. "I had it Fed-Exed from Kyoto."

A waitress shimmied by carrying a tray of sushi. Corwin grabbed a square dish of hot-pink raw fish and held it beneath Bosley's nose. "Blowfish?" he offered.

"Isn't that poisonous?" Bosley asked.

Suddenly he heard Dylan's voice in his ear receiver. "Technically," she said. "One in sixty is fatal."

"It's a rare delicacy," Corwin urged. He leered at Bosley. "For those who don't fear an excruciating death."

Bosley reached for the cold, slimy bit of blowfish with trembling fingers. This stanky fish might be the last thing I ever taste, he thought. Oh, the tragedy! Oh, I never made it to Venice! Oh, I think I left the oven on at home!

Then he placed the sushi in his mouth and chewed slowly, waiting for the poison to spread through him, paralyzing his nervous system, slowing his heart and finally, agonizingly, deflating his tortured lungs.

Um . . . still here.

"Hmmm," Bosley blurted, sighing with relief. "Tastes like chicken."

He laughed loudly. Life, sweet life! he thought.

"It'll go very nice with broccoli," he quipped to Corwin.

"The man laughs at death!" Corwin shouted gleefully. "You remind me of someone else I know."

"And who might that be?" Bosley prodded, leaning forward and opening his mouth to get Corwin's words on tape. Hope I don't have blowfish in my teeth, he thought.

"Why," Corwin said, "Roger Corwin, of course. Finally, a worthy adversary. But let's see if you can survive a test of intuition and judgment. Have you seen the Zen leisure complex?"

"I'm game," Bosley said, with a gulp.

As Corwin led Bosley through the crowd, Bosley said to the air (to his molar mic, actually), "I think we can forget those Hammerheads."

Across the room, Natalie passed some caviar to a shipping magnate and said, "Great work, Bos! Get him to talk about Knox."

A second later, Dylan's voice filled her ear. It was as if she were standing at Natalie's shoulder.

"See any creepy thin men?" she asked.

"Lots of creepy," Natalie replied, glancing at the plastic partiers around her. "No thin."

She hit the bar and set her tray on it.

"*Konichiwa,*" the bartender said.

Natalie glanced up. Whoa. Hottie alert at two o'clock—a brown-haired bartender with brown eyes you could drown in, dimples up the yin-yang, and a name tag that read, Pete. He was wearing a black silk T-shirt and a smile.

"Sugoi desu ne . . . anata wa nihongo o hanusu desu (Wow, that's great. You speak Japanese)," Natalie enthused. She forgot her usual shyness in the presence of a fellow Japanophile.

The bartender returned her smile as he tossed liqueurs and fizzy mixers into glasses without glancing at them once.

"That's incredible," he murmured.

"What is?" Natalie inquired, trying hard to focus on Pete's words and not his chiseled jawline.

"Your smile," Pete answered.

"Thank you," Natalie said, feeling herself turn bright pink. She grabbed her tray, which was now filled with cocktails. Then she ducked back into the swirling crowd.

"What are you doing?" Dylan shrilled in Natalie's ear. "The bartender's cute!"

"I'm working," Natalie protested. As if to prove her point to her buds, who must have been watching her from somewhere nearby, she handed a highball to a portly bald man.

Now it was Alex's voice piping into Natalie's earpiece.

"He likes you," she said. "Go back and flirt a little."

Natalie shook her friends' voices away. But she did

glance over her shoulder to check out Pete once more. He was pouring champagne into slender flutes. And whoa, holy biceps!

Before she could stop and talk herself out of it, Natalie wheeled around and headed back to the bar.

Pete was waiting for her with a big smile. Oh, those dimples, Natalie thought. They're killing me.

"That was fast," Pete said.

Natalie felt her stomach lurch, and she began to back away.

"Well, I can come back later when—"

"No, no," the cutie said. Then he thrust his hand over the bar and smiled again. "I'm Pete."

"That's a nice name," Natalie purred. "I'm Natalie."

"That's a nice name, too," Pete said. "I haven't seen you at any of these things before. Are you new?"

"Yep. Yep," Natalie said, fiddling awkwardly with her kimono sash and blushing again. "I'm brand new. It's my first time . . . here . . . at Corwin's."

Oh. God. Could Natalie be any more of a loser?

"Oh, boy," said Alex's voice in Natalie's ear. "She's going down."

"No way," Dylan protested. "He's into her."

The redheaded Angel had it right. Pete's dimple deepened. He was grinning at Natalie. And he was unbelievably adorable.

"Nat," Alex ordered, "pick up the tray and leave."

"Why?" Natalie blurted.

"I'm sure I wouldn't have forgotten you," Pete said.

"Smile and walk away," Alex instructed.

Regretfully, Natalie began to leave the bar.

"Wait!" Dylan said. "Go back and talk to him."

Natalie did a 180 and faced Pete. Wait, she thought. That's not right. She did another 180 and headed back into the party. Wait! Oh, now she was spinning in circles.

"Flip your hair!" Alex called. She had the same tone of voice one would use to yell, "Grab the life preserver!"

"What?" asked the flustered Natalie.

"Your hair," Alex said. "Flip it. Flip your hair!"

Natalie waved her head in a graceful arc, feeling her blond 'do whirl past her face in a glimmering, shimmering wave. Hair-flipping had been number one on Charlie's training agenda when he'd hired the Angels. A good thing, too.

"Excuse me!"

Natalie turned. Pete—looking breathless and starry-eyed—had turned up at her shoulder.

"I'm sorry," he continued. "I don't usually do this, only, I was wondering . . . that is, unless you're seeing someone else . . ."

"Yes," Natalie blurted.

"You are. Of course you are," Pete said, his face falling. He turned to retreat back to the bar. "I'm sorry—"

"No!" Natalie exclaimed, grabbing his elbow. "I mean . . . I'd love to."

Pete's face broke back into those fabulous dimples. "Great!" he said. "Ah, Thursday?"

"That's my favorite day," Natalie burbled.

"Wow," Pete said. "So, I'll get tickets."

"I love tickets," she cooed. With her stomach fluttering happily, Natalie officially went back to work. In her ear, she heard Alex's voice.

"What are the odds?" she said wryly. "A guy who speaks Natalie."

"Where's J. D.?" Dylan wondered. Natalie scanned the crowd. No sign of Bos.

"He's in Corwin's grotto," Alex said. "Who knows what kind of stuff goes on in there."

CHAPTER

5

October 17, 9:28 P.M.
Location: Corwin's indoor lagoon
Action: Water sports

Marco!"

"Polo!"

Bosley was flailing in a murky black rooftop lagoon with some comely creatures—three babes in bikinis—and Corwin. This was the most vicious game of Marco Polo he'd ever seen. Not that he was seeing it. He was the Marco man, who had to locate his prey with his eyes shut, tracking them from the sound of their voices.

"Marco!" Bosley screamed.

"Polo!" Corwin and the comely creatures taunted.

With his eyes squeezed shut and his mouth hanging open to give his molar mic access, Bosley tried to make casual conversation.

"So . . . Rog," he said, dog-paddling to the area where he thought Corwin might be lurking. "How's business? Competition making you a little crazy? Perhaps, a little desperate? Marco."

"Polo," Corwin yelled, splashing a handful of water into Bosley's open mouth.

Bosley tensed every muscle he had—admittedly, there weren't many—and lunged to his left, connecting to two bodies. One was soft and voluptuous, the other wiry and hairy. Corwin!

"Gotcha!" His eyes snapped open, and he saw Corwin fuming. He hated to be bested at anything, even Marco Polo. To top it off, the blonde in Bosley's grip was calling for an instant replay.

"You got him first," she protested, pointing at Corwin.

"No way," Corwin yelled, splashing her. Then he glared at Bosley.

"Rage," he declared, "we need to settle this mano-a-mano, Japanese style."

October 17, 9:48 P.M.
Location: Back at the party
Quest: Wherefore art thou, Thin Man?

Alex meandered through the crowd, smiling at Natalie, who was standing at the bar. Her bud was drowning in Pete's brown eyes and making small talk in Japanese.

Then Alex scanned the crowd for the elusive Thin Man. She could see Dylan on the opposite side of the courtyard, surrounded by a cluster of tuxedo-clad men.

Alex had to sigh. Drooling admirers were so predictable, but she had badder fish to catch.

Suddenly she got a bite. There was the Thin Man, leaning against a Japanese plum tree. He looked just as he had on the surveillance video—pale and angular with the iciest blue eyes Alex had ever seen. He was smoking a cigarette and gazing absently, contemptuously into the throng.

Alex caught her breath and stifled any sudden movement. She didn't know much about their skinny prey, but she knew he was a consummate pro. One false move and he'd be onto them immediately.

"Murphy O'Meyer! Thin Man at ten o'clock," Alex said into her molar mic. Immediately, she began to drift toward the Thin Man, while Dylan closed ranks as well.

Natalie hurriedly scribbled her number on a napkin and slid it across the bar toward Pete.

"I gotta go," she said, flashing him her toothiest come-hither grin.

Then she joined her fellow Angels.

Let the stalk begin, Natalie thought.

The Thin Man, as if sensing the Angels' presence, snuffed out his cigarette and headed into the lagoon. Then he hit a button hidden in a rock wall.

A black-lacquered shoji panel slid silently into the wall, revealing a short hallway decorated with Japanese calligraphy and fluttering origami cranes.

Natalie—who'd spent the afternoon hacking into city architecture files to download a blueprint of Corwin's penthouse—knew just where the Thin Man was going.

"He's headed for the service elevator," she told her partners.

The trio followed the Thin Man, staying far enough behind him to elude detection, but close enough to see him grab a slender cane from an umbrella stand in a corner. Then he slipped into the elevator. The door hummed shut almost immediately.

Natalie nodded toward an unobtrusive door covered in Japanese rice paper.

"Stairwell," she barked. They raced for the exit.

October 17, 10:04 P.M.
Location: A Sumo sand pit
Observation: Marco Polo was nothing compared to this

Bosley had been in a lot of situations. When the Angels had gone undercover as carnies, he'd been part of the freak show. When they'd pretended to be a rock band, he'd been the roadie. He'd been their drill sergeant in Panama. He'd even dressed in drag.

But this was the limit, he thought. He was facing Roger Corwin in a sand-filled ring, with party guests milling around them. And these guests—so demure, so civilized just a few minutes ago, sipping their bubbly—had been transformed into rabid fans. Fans of Sumo wrestling.

Which meant of course that Bosley and his adversary had been transformed into Sumo wrestlers.

Enormous, unwieldy fat suits, complete with G-strings, black wigs and cellulite (oh, the indignity!) did the trick. Now they were stomping around in the circle and slamming into each other like grunting walruses.

"Marco!" Corwin said in mocking, high-pitched whine. "Polo! Yeah! See if you can beat Roger Corwin at *this* game, fatso!"

Then Corwin bashed Bosley again.

"Noooooo," Bosley called. He was toppling over like a 500-pound Weeble. As he crashed to the sand, he heard Alex's voice piping in his ear.

"Where's J. D.?" she queried. She was puffing a bit, as if she was running or, perhaps, playing hopscotch. Hopscotch, too? Bosley thought. Corwin has gone too far now!

"Ahoy, Jelly Doughnut," Natalie was saying in Bosley's ear. "We need you."

"Uh," Bosley grunted. He lay flailing in his fat suit. He was stuck on his back, as helpless as a tortoise. "This could take just a second."

Then Bosley gasped. Corwin was taking a running start . . .

"I've fallen," Bosley squeaked. Corwin heaved his massive bulk into the air "And I can't get—"

Splat.

Corwin was atop him, squishing every bone in Bosley's body deep into the sand.

"Up," Bosley grunted. He rolled his eyes and scowled. Just call him Boy Blob Bosley.

* * *

October 17, 10:11 P.M.
Location: A stairwell in the Corwin building
Status: Going down at lightning speed

As Alex tore down flight after flight of stairs, with Natalie and Dylan close on her heels, she put a finger in her ear, straining to hear Bosley's voice.

"I've fallen," he was saying, "and I can't get—"
BZGHZZZZ.

The static of Bosley's molar mic shorting out made Alex's head reel. She saw her buds wince, too. Their eyes met. They were on their own now. And they were in a race with the Thin Man's elevator to the bottom of this skyscraper.

As they vaulted down the stairs, Dylan popped a button at her waistline. In one swift motion, she ripped away her dress's long, tight skirt, instantly transforming her gown into pants.

Alex whipped off her bobbed wig and ditched her jewelry.

Natalie's waiter outfit was already action-worthy, but she pulled her hair into a ponytail.

By the time the Angels emerged from the building, they had done a total *"Cosmo* Girl"—transforming from evening togs to workout wear in a flash.

And there was the Thin Man, whose elevator must have stopped on every other floor. He was slinking out of the lobby and scurrying down a dank, narrow alley across the street.

"Why do they always run?" Alex sighed. The Angels began to sprint after him, just as a herd of

Harley-riding bikers blasted down the street and turned down the alley.

The Thin Man loped to a halt and turned to face the girls. A quivering, smarmy smile cracked his lipless mouth.

Something's not right, Dylan thought. An instant later the Thin Man drew his gun and fired, ignoring the noodle shops and tattoo parlors that lined the alley.

"Watch it!" Dylan screamed.

The Angels split up and dove behind whatever shelter each could find. Bullets thunked off the shopfronts and garbage bins. The Angels had no choice but to hunker down and wait until the Thin Man ran out of ammo.

When the shots stopped, they peeked out from their hiding places. The Thin Man was running down the alley, heading for a tall chain-link gate.

Dylan gave her fellow Angels a curt nod and yelled, "Now's our chance!"

They took off after the Thin Man, but he was quick. By the time they reached the gate, he'd already ducked through it and locked it behind him. Dylan grabbed hold of the gate and rattled it in frustration.

But the Angels weren't out of moves. Dylan and Alex locked arms to create a springboard for Natalie. She backed up the alley, then took off at a brisk run and launched herself off the other Angels' arms. Long legs slicing the air, she vaulted over the fence, grabbing a curtain hanging from a laundry line. In a perfect imitation of Tarzan, she swung through the air and knocked over the Thin Man.

He hit the ground hard, then sprang up to kick Natalie in the chest, knocking her through a wooden fence. Where was her backup?

Dylan and Alex were swarming over the chain-link fence, spiderlike. When they landed on the other side, Alex grabbed a broom that was resting against a wall. As the Thin Man prepared to attack Natalie again, Alex swept the handle at his ankles, tripping him.

Again he went down, and again he bounced up. Who was this guy, Rubber Man?

Dylan's turn. She jumped the Thin Man from behind and put him in a choke hold. He spun her around and around, making sure that he knocked her head against a brick wall. Then he grabbed a hank of her hair and yanked hard. And just to show they really weren't going to be friends, he threw her to the ground. Dylan could feel the bruises forming even before she hit.

While the Thin Man was momentarily distracted, Alex scooted down the alley, hugging the wall as she darted along.

But this was no meet and greet. The Thin Man turned and bolted away from the Angels. Dylan and Natalie were right after him. He was just about to emerge from the alley when he had a vision. But it was not a vision he wanted to see—it was an Angel, Alex, blocking his escape. They had him trapped. He'd have to fight.

Moving as one finely tuned machine, the Angels advanced on the Thin Man. They had the moves, and they were going to use them. The Thin Man shifted from foot to foot, trying to anticipate what they were going to do.

In a stream of motion as beautiful as any ballet, Natalie bent forward, and Dylan rolled across her back, kicking. Then Natalie launched herself into a flying kick, bicycling her legs in the air. At the last moment she knocked the Thin Man down.

He was down but not out. He recovered quickly, then scrabbled, crablike, backward on his hands and feet. Alex was just preparing to finish him off when he used his hands to vault himself into a reverse handspring. He landed on his feet and sprinted down the alley, dived into a hidden tunnel—a sort of aboveground sewage drain—and disappeared into the gloom.

The Angels sprinted into the tunnel after their prey. There was a hazy light source somewhere, and they could just make out a door at the end of the tunnel.

The Thin Man didn't seem to be slowing down. His speed only mounted as he approached the door and burst through it.

The Angels piled on some speed of their own and nearly wedged themselves in the doorway as they tried to get through it at the same time.

They were peering down yet another hallway, with yet another door at the end.

No Thin Man.

The Angels charged down the hallway and pummeled down that door.

Then they walked into an eerie room—hazily lit, bare-walled, totally creepy. There was nothing here but a circle of more doors. It was like a sinister funhouse.

Dylan took a deep breath and chose one of the entrances, plunging through with abandon.

She fell into a dirty room with unfinished floors, complete with a skittering rat, a Chinese dragon, and cartons of firecrackers, but no Thin Man. Dylan backed out of the room and slammed the door.

Meanwhile, Natalie was trying door #2. She burst through and screamed. A stony figure leaped out at her. She raised her fists for a fight before she realized she was facing a dressmaker's dummy wearing a Mao jacket. She glanced around the room—more mannequins, rolls of silk, and sewing machines. Natalie laughed dryly.

Alex plunged through door #3, then threw her hands up to her face. A chicken—plumped for slaughter or a cockfight—flew at her face, squawking and angry. Other hens strutted around the feather-littered room, unleashing an unholy noise and stench. But again, no Thin Man.

The Angels glanced at one another.

There was one door left, and they were sure they knew who was lurking behind it.

"One," Dylan whispered.

"Two," Natalie followed.

"Three!" Alex urged.

They kicked the door so hard it flew off its hinges and landed three feet beyond the threshold. Then they crashed into the room, waving away a cloud of dust. They squinted into the dank, windowless room.

A figure was seated in a chair, bound with his hands behind him.

He had floppy brown hair and a ruggedly handsome face. He wore a disheveled tuxedo and two days' worth of scruff, not to mention a few bruises and unwashed, bloody cuts. His mouth was gagged with a strip of dirty cloth.

He gazed at the Angels in fear.

Dylan took a halting step toward the man and stared at him.

"Eric Knox?" she asked.

CHAPTER

6

Eric Knox was sitting on one of the agency's creamy, sleek sofas. He was scruffless and wearing a clean, white polo shirt. His sandy brown hair was just tousled enough to say, Me? A multimillionaire? Big deal.

The buttoned-down-as-ever Vivian Wood was perched on the couch arm, right by Knox's side. She pursed her beige lips at the Angels in a prim simulation of a smile.

Knox shot the Angels a grateful look and said, "They would have killed me if you hadn't shown up when you did. I knew after they stole my code, I was dead meat."

Dylan was over by the blender whipping up a California cocktail—that would be a vitamin-saturated smoothie. She glanced at Knox. Then she cocked her head. There was something about this guy—his pale intensity, his passion, or maybe it was that sexy cut over his left eyebrow. He was, well . . . distracting.

"Now they have full access to my software designs," Knox said, leaping to his feet and pacing in agitation. "It's a disaster waiting to happen."

Alex gazed at Knox with cool confidence.

"We don't let disasters happen, Mr. Knox."

Dylan crossed the floor and handed Knox a glass of something pink and frosty.

"Smoothie?" she said soothingly. "B_6, B_{12}, ginseng. It'll calm you down. Try it."

Knox accepted the drink. His eyes lingered on hers for a moment. Then he flashed Dylan a sweet smile.

Uh-oh, Dylan thought. That's a *nice* smile. She felt a familiar frisson in her belly. Attraction. For the wrong guy, of course. Knox was a client, a strict no-no. She tried to squelch the frisson by going all cold and businesslike. She planted herself on the other sofa next to Natalie, who was questioning Knox.

"So, this software," she said. "Have you written the next killer app and you're worried this might affect an IPO?"

"No," Knox said emphatically, taking a swig of his smoothie. "This isn't about money. This is about the protection of human rights."

Alex and Natalie exchanged an oh-so-furtive skeptical glance. Translation: Another man who thinks he's saving the world. Ho-hum.

"See," Knox explained, "I've developed a program that maps a person's voice. The sound of one's voice is like a fingerprint, a snowflake—totally unique."

Wait a minute—hold that ho-hum, Alex thought.

"So basically you've decoded audio DNA?" she asked.

Knox nodded.

Alex turned to her colleagues and raised her eyebrows.

"That's major," she breathed. Alex was impressed. And *nothing* impressed Alex.

"Corwin's been trying to do it for years," Vivian added. "But we got there first."

"Think about it," Natalie said, her blue eyes flashing with injustice. "Corwin's got Red Star's satellites covering every inch of the planet. If he has this voice ID technology, too, it's the end of privacy, the end of security—"

"Talk about Big Brother," Alex said.

"You're right, Alex."

That was Charlie on the speakerphone. He'd been listening in silence to this whole exchange, but now it was time for him to take the reins.

"In the wrong hands," Charlie observed, "this could be very dangerous."

"Lucky for us, Corwin invited John David Rage to the time trials for his Dash for Cash charity race," Bosley said, his already puffy chest puffing just a tad more with pride. "While they 'dash for the cash,' we'll 'search through his trash.' "

Bosley leaned back in his office chair and grinned. He'd swung a major undercover coup *and* formulated the perfect pun. What a morning he was having!

Charlie jumped in with his marching orders.

"Natalie and Alex, come up with a way to get into

Red Star," he said. "In the meantime, Dylan, you're in charge of Mr. Knox's security. I'd hate to have him kidnapped again."

Suddenly, Dylan's pointy-toed black boots became very interesting to her. She could feel her cheeks flushing slightly.

Then she scolded herself. He's just a *guy*. He's nothing. Snap out of it, Dylan.

She shook her head slightly and looked up.

"Absolutely," she said in a cool, controlled voice. "But we'd all feel safer if you could join us, Charlie."

"I'd love to, Angels," squawked the speaker. "But I'm in a bit over my head at the moment."

Then, Dylan heard an odd, eerie sound: an underwater burble and the hiss of a scuba diver's oxygen tank.

Just where was Charlie anyway? The forbidden question was on the tip of Dylan's tongue. She just *had* to know. But before the words could escape her lips, the speakerphone went dead.

As always, Dylan felt an emptiness sweep through her when the connection was broken.

"So long, Charlie," she whispered.

Then she turned briskly to Knox and said, "Let's begin a security sweep, shall we? Might as well start with your car. Tonight we'll hit your house."

She grabbed her jacket and stalked out the door. Knox glanced at Alex and Natalie for a moment, raised one eyebrow, à la Dylan, and scampered after her.

October 18, 7:29 P.M.
Location: Eric Knox's mansion, Laurel Canyon
Wardrobe: Emotional guard, up and ready

Dylan had cleared Knox to drive his own muscle car. Then she'd driven to his house in her own orange-and-white Camaro.

Chez Knox was a gleaming, cliffside manse of the oh-so-modern variety. It was round—like a flying saucer—very space-age steel and glass, very *Architectural Digest,* very nouveau multimillionaire.

When they went inside, the two of them stood awkwardly for a minute. Dylan took a look around. The interior of the house sported an open plan, with one space flowing into the next.

Then Dylan blurted, "Skylights! My guess is they would be—" She pointed toward the ceiling.

"Follow me," Knox said. They crossed through the living area. It was all boxy couches and loveseats, a few tasteful, geometric end tables, some soft lighting—the well-crafted works. Dylan tossed her jacket on a couch as they headed for an interior door. One bare corridor later, they were looking up at a portal in the ceiling.

"How about a boost?" Dylan said.

Knox just grinned and cupped his hands. In a second Dylan was standing on Knox's broad shoulders, scanning the window with a bug-and-bomb-detecting laser device.

"Nothing up here," she called down.

"Here, let me give you a hand," Knox offered.

But Dylan beat him to the punch, doing a reverse pull-up and dropping to the floor next to Knox.

"Or not," Knox said with an impressed grin.

Wow, Dylan thought, I didn't know they *made* teeth that white. She shook that pesky frisson away and began a brisk sweep of the entire house, including Knox's bedroom.

Not exactly cozy, Dylan thought, gazing at the big empty space. There was nothing but a bed with a tight, flat coverlet, a wind-up alarm clock and phone on the floor, and a killer view of the canyon.

Dylan made a beeline for the phone and began dismantling it in a hunt for bugs.

As she skimmed through her detective work, Dylan spied a lone, silver picture frame tucked close to the bed. She picked it up. The frame held a yellowed snapshot of two men in camouflage. They wore grass-colored berets over close-cropped hair. From the lurid color of the photo, Dylan dated it around 1975. One of the men had beautiful teeth and warm brown eyes, just like Knox's. The other must have been laughing when the shutter opened. His face was a blur.

"Who are the Green Berets?" Dylan asked.

"My dad," Knox replied. He gazed affectionately, almost intensely, at the photo in Dylan's hand.

"That's sweet," Dylan said breezily.

Then Knox's voice turned grim.

". . . and the man who killed him," he added.

"What?" Dylan blurted.

Knox walked away from her. He gazed out the

window at the canyon's boulders, glinting in the morning sunshine.

"They were in army intelligence together," he explained quietly. "My father's best friend—he turned on him."

"I'm so sorry," Dylan murmured. She looked at the photo with new eyes, then gazed at the back of Knox's head quizzically. "Why do you keep it?"

"To remind me," he replied, "be careful who you trust."

Dylan gave a dry, little laugh. So true. And so close to her own philosophy in life.

Knox tried to lighten the mood by turning to Dylan and asking, "So what about you? Parents?"

Tough question. Dylan was silent for a moment. Then she headed for the living room with Knox on her heels. She flopped into one of his sumptuous leather couches and said, "My mother died when I was little. I never met my father."

"Never met your father," Knox mused, alighting on the couch next to her. "Now you work for a man you've never met. Interesting trend."

Knox took her hand and leaned toward her. It seemed like the most natural move in the world, client or no.

Knox entwined his fingers with Dylan's. His skin was so smooth. When he squeezed her fingers, a warm little zip went all the way up to her elbow.

Dylan squeezed back—for what seemed a very long time. She wondered if his lips were as soft as his hands. They were so close. . . .

Dylan shook her head and leaped to her feet. Close one, she thought. I've got to get out of here.

She walked briskly into the kitchen, after grabbing her jacket off the couch and slipping it on. Knox followed her as if in a trance. From her pocket Dylan pulled a rodlike device with a red button on one end.

"Before I leave, let me give you this," she said, tossing the rod over her shoulder to Knox. "It's a panic button. Any problems, just press it and whoever is closest will be here immediately."

"Right now, that would be you," Knox said. He pressed the red button, then looked up at Dylan with a flirty grin.

"Yes, but Mr. Knox," Dylan said coyly, "I don't think you have a problem right now." She leaned against an island in the center of the kitchen,

"Yeah, I do," Knox countered, crossing to the pantry and pulling a box of Shake 'n Bake from a shelf. "I don't know how to make chicken."

Dylan couldn't help but smile. That line was so terrible, it was charming. She played along.

"I'll shake," she said, slipping her jacket off again. "You bake?"

"Nah," Knox said, crossing over to Dylan. "I wanna shake."

October 18, 8:04 P.M.
Location: Eric Knox's kitchen
Status: The heat is on

Before Dylan knew what was happening, they were listening to an old Leo Sayer album on a record player. Dylan was chopping vegetables at the island, while Knox put a chicken leg into a Ziploc bag filled with Shake 'n Bake. He gave the bag a flirty little shake and passed it to Dylan.

Their fingers touched.

Whoa, Dylan thought. It was as if a jolt of electricity had thrummed through her. She looked up at Knox and felt her eyes lock with his, warm pools of chocolate brown . . .

She shook her head and refocused on the celery she was chopping. Then she heard another shake. Knox was handing over another bag of chicken.

She reached for the bag. And then Knox's hand was on hers. They dropped the bag and let their fingers come together.

In an instant, his lips were on hers. The kiss was so soft that at first, it felt like a daydream. Then Knox pressed harder. Dylan's lips were tingling. She melted into the kiss, leaning back against the island. The chopping board and various veggies tumbled to the floor but Dylan barely noticed. She didn't care. Every brain cell she had was wrapped around Knox's soft, soft lips.

But then a jar of something—pickles?—that she'd kicked out of her way rolled across the floor and bumped into the record player. The needle skittered across the Leo Sayer album with a painful scratching sound. Dylan's eyes flew open, and she was jolted back to reality.

And in reality, she was wrapped in her client's arms. There was a carrot gouging her back and her Angel code of honor was trashed.

Dylan lurched up.

"Uhh, I should actually . . . go," she blurted.

Knox helped her off the table, looking as bleary-eyed as Dylan felt.

"You are a client, and—" she said.

Dylan grabbed her jacket and headed to the front door, smoothing her tousled hair and trying to get hold of herself. Knox just smiled at her helplessly—he was clearly smitten.

Dylan turned around as she hit the door. She was sorely tempted to launch herself back into Knox's arms. But instead she said, "I should go. And I will. Go. Now."

Dylan couldn't help but smile at Knox's adorable grin.

"Enjoy your dinner, Mr. Knox," she said, opening the door. "And don't forget to lock the door behind me."

She rushed away. Once outside, she leaned against the front door, biting her lip—which was still tingling. Dylan realized she was toying with the door-knob, imagining going back inside, going back to him. . . .

She dashed to her car. In a fit of frustration, she gunned the motor and peeled out.

CHAPTER

7

October 19, Noon
Location: The Dash for Cash time trials, Los Angeles
    County Dragway
Wardrobe: Built for distraction

You there, little miss. Careful with those lugnuts,"
Bosley ordered, snapping his fingers at Alex.

He was playing, no, he *was* John David Rage, over-
seeing a beautiful "team of mechanics" working on
"his racecar." They were in a trackside maintenance
pit at the L.A. Dragway. All around them actual racers were preparing for the speed trial of the season.

Alex gave Bosley a baleful look.

"Watch it," she warned him playfully. "Better yet,
watch Corwin."

That was easy to do. Corwin was in the next pit.
Every once in a while, the magnate glanced over to
leer at the Angels in their costumes.

They wore skin-tight, royal blue jumpsuits with
red piping and white stars, tinted aviator shades, and
wigs. Natalie had been transformed into a sultry
brunette. Dylan wore a platinum mane with flipped-

back wings—a 'do she'd seen on some TV show from the '70s.

The Angels peered back at Corwin. He looked sleazy as ever in a garishly colored silk shirt. A cut-crystal glass of Scotch on the rocks tinkled in his hand.

As Corwin's car was readied for the race, he schmoozed with an assortment of barrel-chested big-wigs and hangers-on.

"When Roger Corwin first got involved in racing," he told them, "a lot of people thought it was just a rich man's fancy. Well, I had those people fired."

Raucous laughter rippled through the hangers-on.

"What's so funny?" he sputtered. "I did. I wish I could fire some of you!" He gulped down another mouthful of Scotch.

Dylan rolled her eyes at Alex.

"He's going nowhere," she muttered. "Let's do it." The pair began to skulk away from the track. As they went, Dylan heard Corwin saying, "Thanks for showing up for the time trials. I guarantee tomorrow's race and all this weekend's festivities will be even better. Then I guess it's back to the day-to-day grind of world domination and enslavement. Can't wait."

Oh, *blech,* Dylan thought, curling her lip.

"There it is," Alex murmured. Dylan followed her bud's gaze to a gorgeous silver Bentley Arnage hogging three handicapped parking spots near the track. A vanity license plate beneath the grill read, COR-WIN.

Alex ducked behind another car and nodded to Dylan.

"Go, girl," she urged.

Dylan took a deep breath, pasted on a Barbie-esque toothy smile, and opened the Bentley's passenger door.

October 19, 12:11 P.M.
Location: Roger Corwin's Bentley. Interior
Mission: Subterfuge via seduction

Dylan plopped into the car next to the uniformed chauffeur, who'd been lounging behind the wheel, listening to Dr. Laura.

He jumped.

"What the—" the chauffeur began. Then he took in Dylan—all of Dylan, from her low-cut jumpsuit to her red-lacquered nails. He fell silent, his eyes bugging out.

Dylan clicked off the radio, batted her eyelashes at the chauffeur, and fanned her hand in front of her face.

"My, it's hot out there!" she exclaimed in a Marilyn Monroe-breathy voice. "Oh, but it's so hot in here, too."

"Let me see if I can make you more comfortable," the chauffeur said, turning up the air conditioning. Dylan arched her back and leaned over the vent, letting the cool air flutter her blond wings around her cheeks.

She winked at the chauffeur. "Thanks," she purred.

October 19, 12:14 P.M.
Location: Roger Corwin's Bentley. Exterior
Gear: A contraband key and a hidden camera

Alex crouched behind the Bentley and peeked through the small, rear window. Dylan was flirting hard—she could tell from her body language. She saw the chauffeur flick some sweat off his brow. He was biting, big-time.

Eew, Alex thought.

Alex took the key they'd filched from Madame Wong's out of her pocket. Then she popped the trunk and found Corwin's briefcase. It was made of soft, black, Italian leather. Reaching into her own bag, Alex selected a black leather sheath and slipped it over the briefcase handle. Then she held the handle up to her eye and adjusted a tiny glass bubble imbedded in the leather.

"A microscopic video camera, complete with fisheye lens," Alex murmured admiringly. "Gotta love it."

She tossed the briefcase back into the trunk, pocketed the key, and strolled away.

October 19, 12:15 P.M.
Location: Roger Corwin's Bentley. Interior
Mantra: Avoid getting trapped in one's own web

Dylan glanced at her watch. She figured Alex needed about four minutes to get the job done. It had been three minutes. She sighed inwardly and turned back to the chauffeur. Ick—did he have to drool?

Dylan hid her disgust and cooed, "I love cars."

The chauffeur leaned toward her. Dylan pressed her back against her window. Who decided to make Bentleys so small, she wondered.

"Do you like *fast* cars?" the chauffeur said.

"Speaking of which—" Dylan blurted. Then she pointed at the racetrack, where the race had just kicked off. "Looks like the race has started. I've got to get back to work. Thanks for the ride."

She burst out of the Bentley with a sigh of relief, just as Alex closed the car's trunk and strolled away. Gratefully, Dylan trotted after her.

October 19, 12:13 P.M.
Location: John David Rage's pit, Los Angeles County
     Dragway
Gear: Hot wheels

As Alex and Dylan slunk around Roger Corwin's Bentley, Natalie joined the group around Corwin. With half her brain she managed to distract him from his ego-tripping speeches in her best flirtatious manner.

With the other half of her brain Natalie gazed at the race and sighed happily. She'd be in heaven if she weren't so focused on the Corwin case. Well, she was also focused on the tar track, shimmering with heat. And the racers in their satin suits. And that fabulous gasoline aroma . . . And, oh yeah, the Corwin case.

Speaking of which, there was the Red Star racer pulling into the pit now. Natalie admired the sleek red roadster. She walked over and leaned in to take a peek at the interior.

The Red Star driver took a peek at her. Or, more to the point, he glared at her with a murderous scowl and some chillingly pale blue eyes.

The Thin Man!

The thug saw right through Natalie's costume. He pointed at her, narrowed his eyes, and gunned his motor. In an instant, he was outta there.

Before she could stop to think, Natalie was racing to the blue roadster parked in Bosley's pit. She slipped on a helmet with two-way radio connection and hopped into the car.

She set her sights on the Red Star racer, then gunned her motor and peeled out.

October 19, 12:16 P.M.
Location: Trackside at the Dash for Cash
Status: Quitting time? Not even . . .

Alex and Dylan were sauntering back to the track after planting the camera on Corwin's briefcase. They gave each other a subdued high-five and grinned.

"Mission accomplished," Alex said. "Tomorrow morning Corwin's giving us a guided tour of Red Star."

Dylan gazed out at the track happily. But her smile faded quickly. She pointed with a trembling finger at their pit.

Alex followed Dylan's gaze and saw the Thin Man, glaring out of the Red Star racer. Then she saw Natalie hop into the Angels' racer. An instant later, their bud was going 220 miles per hour around a dragway, locked in an endless, vicious pursuit.

"Natalie!" the two Angels shouted. They raced to the side of the track and threw on their headsets.

"Natalie!" Dylan yelled into her mic. "Stay back."

"It's a round track," Alex urged. "He's not going anywhere."

October 19, 12:18 P.M.
Location: The Dash for Cash
Status: The big chase scene

Alex's words were echoing in Natalie's helmet.

Natalie bit her lip. Her compadres were right. Where could the Thin Man go? It would be safer to pull back.

But then she saw, out of the corner of her eye, a splash of red. It was car number eleven. Inside, the Thin Man curled his lip at her. Then he ground his gears and passed her.

All practicality and safety measures flew out of Natalie's head. "No way you're passing me, you skinny punk," she muttered. She floored it.

That's when the Thin Man jumped the track. He blasted out of the dragway through an entrance tunnel.

Natalie pulled a hard right. She could feel the asphalt skitter dangerously under her tires, but she just gripped the wheel harder and sailed after her prey.

Natalie tailed the red car, not giving an inch. They sped through an access tunnel and emerged onto a thoroughfare. This being L.A., it was choked with Beamers, minivans, and spring water delivery trucks.

The Thin Man threw his racer into a spin and then shot up the street, going against traffic. He ran red lights, sideswiped cars, and came within inches of pancaking some pedestrians.

Natalie gritted her teeth and glared at the speeding red racer. I'd do a lot to solve a case, she thought, as she wove expertly around traffic islands, baby carriages, and crosswalk guards. But I will not break traffic laws. There, I put my foot down.

Her heart began to palpitate as she approached a red light. The Thin Man blasted through it, causing a three-car pileup—a cacophony of screeching tires and crunching metal.

Natalie glared at the light. Turn green, she meditated. Turn. Green.

"It's not gonna turn," she wailed. "I'll have to stop. I'll lose him!"

The light turned green.

Natalie grinned.

"Right on schedule," she crowed. Then she gasped. "Oh!" she gasped. "Oh, no!"

"What's wrong?" Dylan's voice asked in her helmet's radio receiver.

"I have a date with Pete," Natalie whimpered. She

steered the racer around a stalled Saturn and added, "Right now."

"I think he'll give you a second chance," Alex yelled.

"Nooo," Natalie groaned. Absently, she noticed the Thin Man's racer hopping off the busy street. He scuttled down a steep, grassy divider and skidded onto an access road. Natalie followed with a few quick turns of her wheel and grinding of gears. She was neck and neck with the Thin Man, but all she could do was bite her lip sadly.

"I saw the way he was looking at you," Dylan insisted. "Call him. Trust me."

Natalie banged the steering wheel in annoyance. She glared at the Thin Man, speeding beside her.

"This is all your fault!" she yelled.

Then she glanced back at the road in front of her.

Oh, darn, Natalie thought. On top of everything else, there *would* be an eighteen-wheeler barreling right toward us in a totally narrow tunnel, with no room for escape.

The truck honked at the race cars and flashed its lights urgently. Natalie pressed harder on the gas, hoping to psych out the Thin Man. But he merely kept her pace and glared back at her.

At the last possible moment, Natalie cut her wheel hard to the left.

The Thin Man went right.

Natalie careened up an embankment, going airborne.

"Yahoo!" she screamed. It was almost worth missing her date for such a wild ride.

When she landed with a crash, she saw the Thin Man heading down an unpaved road. She raced after him, but his car kicked up a cloud of throat-choking dust.

Natalie began hacking and swiping at her watery eyes. When the cloud cleared, she'd lost him.

Natalie inched her car forward, searching . . . searching . . .

Well, what do you know. There he was. The Red Star racer was poised at the end of a long narrow bridge. A one-laner. This is where the chase was going to end.

Natalie could hear the Thin Man gun his motor.

She gunned her motor right back.

She tightened her seat harness and revved her engine higher.

He upped his gearage, too.

This is like a dance, Natalie thought. But sorry, buddy, my dance card's full. Then she cranked it.

And so did he.

She sped up.

And so did he.

Neither one of them had any intention of stopping.

Natalie didn't even flinch when they hit. She knew something the Thin Man didn't. Her car was built with the lowest suspension known to racing. It was a test model, brand-new to the market. That meant—if Natalie's instant calculations were correct—her car's nose would hit an inch beneath his, scooping his car into the air and leaving hers untouched.

That's just what happened.

The red car flew into the air as if launched from a catapult. Flipping over Natalie's car, it spun in an almost graceful arc off the bridge.

Natalie slammed on her brakes. Her car skidded, leaving a trail of thick, black smudges on the pavement. Just before it teetered off the bridge, it came to a shuddering halt.

Natalie tossed off her harness and leaped out of the car. She ran to the bridge railing and gazed into the water. She saw no trace of the Red Star racer—only a widening oil slick and a few bubbles.

This dance, Natalie thought, is over.

CHAPTER

October 20, 10:06 A.M.
Location: Charles Townsend Detective Agency
Wardrobe: A day-after-the-first-kiss blush

Dylan willed herself not to look at Eric Knox. But ever since he had walked into the agency a few minutes ago, she'd felt as if there was a magnetic force between them. Even the presence of that icy suit, Vivian Wood, couldn't put a chill on the hot vibes coursing between them.

Even worse, Natalie and Alex could sense those vibes, too. Dylan spotted them shooting each other a look that clearly said, "Uh-oh—client crush alert."

Natalie leaped at the opportunity to diffuse the tension.

"Let's see what Corwin and his magic briefcase handle picked up for us, shall we?" she said. She hit a button on a remote control to close the blinds and lower the plasma screen. Then she started up the remote video input player.

She angled her head to examine the first image that flickered onto the screen.

"Engineers," Alex said, yawning. "All they wear are Dockers."

The camera peeled itself away from a bevy of backsides and caught an overhead security camera. Then a pale finger punched a security code into a keypad. Bosley, who was sitting at his desk, wrote down the sequence.

As they watched Corwin move through a series of increasingly bizarre security measures, Knox shook his head and sighed.

"Red Star's security system is incredible," he said. "I have to say, it seems like they've thought of, well, everything."

"Restricted access," Alex listed.

"Fingerprint ID," Natalie noted.

"Retinal scanner," Dylan added.

"And check that out," Alex said, pointing to a small room on the screen. *"Everything* at Red Star goes through the mainframe, and there's no way to access that database from outside. What's more, only two people at Red Star can get into the mainframe and they have to be together to do it."

"And once we do get the data, it could take days to search all those files," Dylan added.

"It sounds impossible," Vivian said, shaking her head.

The Angels caught one another's glances and couldn't suppress a mutual smirk. They chorused, "Sounds like fun."

October 20, 12:30 P.M.
Location: Zazou Zazou, a Middle Eastern
    restaurant/"entertainment" venue in Hollywood
Wardrobe: Purdahrama

Of course, some people's idea of fun is different from others'. Natalie, for one, was *not* having the time of her life bumping, grinding, and belly-dancing her way around Zazou Zazou.

But that's where Mel Lanzer, a high-level Red Star director, spent most of his lunch hours. And today, while he was shoveling in the $5.99 falafel buffet and more than a few Buds, he was giving "the new girls" an appreciative once-over. As planned.

Natalie wore a red spangled bra and shimmering mesh skirt. She sashayed over to Lanzer and gave her outfit a jingly shake. Yuck, she thought. Does he have to pant?

She danced over to Alex, who wore a gold sequined halter and a long blond wig.

"Remind me why we're doing this?" Natalie begged.

Alex leaned over and whispered, "The mainframe is protected by a failsafe to prevent tampering. Only *that* guy's fingerprint can override it."

The Angels glared at the tipsy, red-faced wonk with the Red Star badge. He smiled at them woozily. Then he waved at a waitress.

" 'Nother Bud," he slurred.

"Of course," said a veiled woman, extending a lace-gloved hand for his empty beer bottle. As Dylan walked away, she furtively slipped the bottle into a plastic bag and tucked it beneath her long veil.

"Sucker," she muttered.

October 20, 2:08 P.M.
Location: Charles Townsend Detective Agency
Gadgetry: State of the art

"I love it when Charlie buys us new toys," Alex said, slipping Lanzer's beer bottle into a cradle and aiming a laser at it. While Natalie and Dylan ditched their spangles and Mata Hari makeup, Alex flipped a switch.

A red laser scanned the face of the bottle and picked out a perfect fingerprint. With a series of whirrs and clicks, a nearby computer digitized the print. Then a printing mold dripped molten rubber onto a finger-shaped stylus.

By the time the Angels had changed into their costumes for their next gig, Dylan was holding a thin, rubbery film in a pair of tweezers—a perfect replica of Mel Lanzer's fingerprint.

"We've got our manicure," she said. "Now let's go get our eyes done."

October 20, 5:48 P.M.
Location: Home of Kenneth McIntyre, high-level Red Star
**   director. Encino**
Wardrobe: High Swiss camp

Kenneth McIntyre was loosening his tie and shrugging out of his suit jacket when he answered the doorbell of his suburban manse.

But when he got a load of his visitors, he stopped. And stared.

Were they decked out in slinky gowns? Extreme Avon lady makeup? Nah—too predictable. You want to make an impression, you show up in braids, embroidered blouses, red knee socks—a whole Swiss Miss cocoa kind of ensemble. Behind them, Bosley, in a pair of lederhosen, was puffing on a tuba.

"*Guten Tag!*" Dylan chirped, batting her eyelashes at McIntyre.

Natalie turned to Dylan, whose million petticoats under her brown dress rustled loudly.

"*Guten Morgen!*" she corrected.

Alex shook her finger at Natalie. "*Guten Nacht!*" she said.

Then they all squealed, "*Guten Freund!*"

Oompah, oooooompah, belched the tuba.

The Angels spent the next ten minutes yodeling and telling German jokes about a too-curious goat and his worried mistress. The Red Star executive was, in a word, transfixed.

So was McIntyre's buddy, who'd sidled up behind him, outfitted for an evening tennis match.

As Natalie launched into a perfect yodel, Dylan handed McIntyre a fancy envelope, a "telegram." The tennis buddy glanced at the envelope clutched in McIntyre's hand.

"They got the wrong address," he hissed.

"Shut up," McIntyre hissed back.

Natalie screwed up her face as she yodeled with her hand to her mouth.

"More loud!" she demanded, pumping her fists up and down.

Dylan raised her finger, then skipped over to Bosley's tuba. She yodeled into the gargantuan bell of the horn. The yodel echoed loudly.

"Ah-ha," Natalie cried. She skipped to the tuba and yodeled into it as well.

Then they offered the tuba to McIntyre. Grinning doggishly, he stuck his face into the tuba and yodeled.

Gotcha, Dylan thought.

October 20, 5:59 P.M.
Location: Dylan's Camaro
Motto: No costume is too humiliating—if it gets the job done

As soon as they'd obtained McIntyre's yodel, the Angels and Bosley had hightailed it out of Encino. Now they were crammed uncomfortably in Dylan's little Camaro. Bosley's tuba emitted a couple of guttural belches as he reached in and extracted a small black box.

"Let's see if the retinal scanner worked," he said, passing the device to Alex. She flipped up a plastic cover on the box, typed some numbers into a keypad, and gave her fellow Angels a thumbs-up.

"It's in," she announced. "All we need to do is head back to the office to craft this into a contact lens with our laser scanner."

"But we still have to get *into* Red Star HQ," Natalie said, "and no one gets through the front door without an invitation."

"She's right," Dylan said, speeding the car back toward the agency with her usual law-bending flair. "How are we going to pull *that* off?"

Alex pulled a pair of black spectacles out of her poufy Swiss Miss skirt pocket and said, "We just walk right in."

October 21, 9:01 A.M.
Location: Red Star Systems' desert headquarters
Mission: B & E, Angel-style

The workday was officially one minute old. Alex stalked into Red Star Systems with her specs perched on the bridge of her nose, and her two assistants in tow. Her assistants were slight men with wispy facial hair. They were quite pretty men. In fact, they bore a striking resemblance to Dylan Sanders and Natalie Cook.

Alex, meanwhile, was crisp and coifed, and she wasn't suffering fools gladly.

Ah, here's one now, she thought dryly. A harried woman in a floral dress—as frowzy as Alex was sleek—rushed up.

"You must be Ms. Aarons," the woman said, thrusting out her hand. "I'm Doris."

Alex ignored Doris's hand and began walking. Briskly, she made her way into a maze of cubicles.

"I-I'm sorry for all this confusion," Doris stuttered as she struggled to keep up with Alex's long strides. "I had you on the schedule for *next* week. Instead of *this* week. I'm usually very good about these things. I don't know what happened."

"That's what I'm here to figure out," Alex said in a clipped voice.

Doris smiled through gritted teeth. "You *are* the efficiency expert," she said.

"Yes," Alex replied coldly. "I am."

Alex continued to stalk quickly through the offices, but the demoralized Doris slowed and then stopped. She glared at Alex's ramrod-straight back.

"Witch," she mouthed.

"I heard that," Alex called over her shoulder.

October 21, 9:11 A.M.
Location: Red Star HQ
Weapon: Efficiency seminar

Alex marched into the conference room. She was followed by an army of guys in wrinkled khakis and polo shirts. There was a lot of mouth breathing and Bill Gates hair going on.

Alex slapped a diagram of the programming department onto an overhead projector.

"Your methodologies are antiquated and weak," she announced. "Your procedures of approval ensure that only the least radical ideas are rewarded. Meanwhile, your competition is innovating."

She pointed to one wrinkly-shirted guy.

"You," she said. "What's your name?"

"Phillip Roach," the geek said, practically swooning.

"What was the last suggestion you made to your boss?" Alex asked.

"I, uh, I thought the Coke machines should be free," he stammered.

"Why?" Alex queried coolly.

"Because caffeine helps us program," Roach said.

Alex squinted at him. She took off her glasses and folded her arms. After a pause, she said, "Perfect. It's smart, simple, and logical. What did your boss say?"

"He said no," Roach replied.

"Question," Alex said, pacing the front of the room. "Who builds the products of this company? You do. Engineers do, not managers. They should be answering to you, not you to them."

"Yeah!" barked one of the geeks, pumping his fist in the air.

"Eeep," gulped Doris.

"Who else has an idea like this man's Coke machine?" Alex asked.

A dozen pale hands shot into the air.

"All right, tell me," Alex said. She gazed around the room and changed her mind.

"Better yet, show me . . ."

October 21, 9:39 A.M.
Location: Programming hub, Red Star HQ
Mission: Distraction

Phillip Roach typed his security code into a keypad. Then he threw open the door to the heavily locked-down programming hub—a room humming with computers. Getting through that door had been the first in a string of obstacles facing the Angels. All three of them breathed silent sighs of relief.

None of the techies had a clue. They were too busy scampering around Alex like puppies, showing her the too-slow firewires that cramped their style and the Byte Me sign that had been confiscated by some suit.

Meanwhile, Dylan and Natalie, a.k.a. Louie and Frank, slipped away from the group. They'd both committed blueprints of Red Star to memory, so they knew exactly where to go. They walked in casual, manly strides through a few twisting, turning hallways and finally came to the security door outside the mainframe room.

Dylan plunged her index finger into a square of neon green gelatinous material in the wall—the fingerprint scanner. She held her breath as she watched a laser skim over her finger, or rather, the fake, rubber print on her finger. In a second, a green light next to the scanner blinked: Approved.

Natalie grinned and stepped up to the next security block—the retinal scanner. Placing her chin on a plastic bar, she opened her eye wide while a mechanical arm gripped her head. Then two sharp, conical shafts sped out of the wall, straight for her pupil. Natalie cringed, but the shafts halted a millimeter from her eyeball. A laser shot a quick, undetectable blast of light into her eye.

The mechanical arm loosened its grip on her head and Natalie pulled away. Glad that's over, she thought. Then she gasped—a red light was blinking next to the retinal scanner: Denied.

Dylan whispered, "Try again."

Natalie blinked several times and submitted to the scanner once more.

Beep. Beep. Beep. Denied.

The red light blinked like a reproachful snake eye. Natalie glanced at Dylan in a silent panic, but Dylan was gazing down the hall.

A mini electric car was cruising toward them, driven by a smarmy man in black: Roger Corwin.

Dylan calculated that they had 3.5 seconds before Corwin would notice them.

"Bathroom," she whispered. They made a beeline for the ladies'. Just before she opened the door, Natalie slapped a hand on her fuzzy goatee. Wrong room! She spun around and ducked into the men's room. Dylan was right behind her.

They were loitering by the sinks when Corwin sauntered in and positioned himself in front of a urinal.

Dylan shot Natalie a glance. Standing around a men's room with nothing to do looked suspicious. Natalie took a deep breath and stalked over to the urinal next to Corwin. Dylan grabbed the one on his other side.

"Did'ya see that new quartzium processor?" Natalie grunted in her best basso growl. "It's amazing."

"Yeah," Dylan replied, doing a gravelly tenor. "It's so tiny."

"Yeah," Natalie echoed, shooting Corwin a glance.

He was zipping up. Then he scowled and stalked to a sink, rinsing quickly before he slammed out of there.

Natalie and Dylan dissolved into giggles before they remembered where they were and what they looked like. Then they harumphed, gave each other punches to the biceps, and headed back out into the hallway. Natalie looked at her watch and tensed up. They didn't have a second to lose.

She stepped up to the retinal scanner and took a deep breath.

She blinked several times. Hard.

Then she rested her chin on the plastic bar and succumbed for a third, agonizing time to the laser blast.

Dylan held her breath.

Natalie emitted a tiny squeak.

Then the light flashed next to the scanner. A green light. With a bell-like chime, it read, Approved.

The door slid open. Natalie turned to Dylan and whispered, "Okay, I'll install the high-speed wireless relay. It'll patch us directly into the mainframe . . ."

". . . and beam the data back to us by microwave," Dylan said. "They'll have no idea we're peeking inside."

"You go back and cover me," Natalie breathed. "I'll need ten minutes. Tops."

Then she ducked into a darkened passageway and watched Dylan's manly figure disappear behind the sliding door.

October 21, 9:58 A.M.
Location: Red Star's mainframe computer room
Wardrobe: White is the new black

Natalie approached the first obstacle before the mainframe—a long, brightly lit white hallway with a security camera at every corner. Before she reached the threshold she reached into her briefcase.

"Time to lighten up," she whispered. She ditched her guy clothes and slipped into a glaringly white body suit. It covered her entire head, her hands, and her feet. A small white mesh window gave her a limited line of vision.

She slunk into the white hallway. She knew Dylan was in the security hub, eyeing the video monitors. And on those monitors—unless something went gravely wrong—Natalie would blend into the walls as seamlessly as a smudge of white paint. She was invisible.

At the end of the hallway, Natalie pushed a button. A glass door whispered open. She stepped through and found herself in a small, square chamber—empty but for two large buttons, one red and one blue, on opposite walls. The door slid closed behind her. Natalie eyed the door exiting the chamber and hit the red button. Then she hit the blue button.

Nothing.

She reversed the order, hitting the blue button first.

Still nothing.

Natalie realized the buttons had to be pressed simultaneously, but they were six feet away from each other. Natalie was tall, lanky, and lithe, but there was no way her arms spanned six feet.

Natalie blew a wisp of blond hair out of her eyes and pondered the problem for about two seconds before she thought of a solution.

Planting one foot on the floor, she extended her leg backward in a horizontal arabesque. Her toe hit the red button. Then she bent at the waist and stretched her fingertips toward the blue button. She could just touch it with her index finger. She pushed both buttons and watched the second door slide open with an electronic sigh.

There it was—the mainframe, an enormous white cube humming in a round room. Natalie caught her breath. She'd heard about this kind of computer but had never seen one with her own eyes.

She was just about to touch the cube when a red glint in the farthest corner of her peripheral vision stopped her cold.

She peered at the base of the wall. Hidden in the crease between the wall and floor were a series of red lasers. They formed an intersecting security fence around the mainframe. If Natalie broke those beams, the entire corporation would go into lockdown. She'd be busted.

From the angle of the laser sources, Natalie surmised that the beams hit the mainframe at every height from zero to five feet.

Natalie took a deep breath. She backed up a few steps. Then she took a running leap, doing a full flip in the air and landing in a crouch on top of the main-frame. She shot a quick glance at the laser sources—they were still working. As far as the boys in security knew, there had been no breach.

Natalie quickly found the access port she was looking for and pried it open with a small screwdriver.

As soon as the port opened, the mainframe began to shudder. The cube unfurled like some giant, robotic lotus blossom, expanding and breaking open to fill the room. Natalie gasped in awe—this was some machine! She clung to the mainframe's top surface until the movement stopped. Then she zoned in on her point of entry, a Gothic-looking circuit board with about a thousand tiny wires protruding from it.

Natalie reached into a pocket and pulled out a custom-built device. In two minutes she had a relay transmitter hooked to the system. All she had to do now was get out.

"And that," Natalie whispered as she leaped off the mainframe, "is what you call efficiency."

October 21, 4:48 P.M.
Location: Knox Technologies, outdoor cafeteria
Status: In like Flynn

By that afternoon a huge chunk of Red Star's data had been downloaded onto Bosley's laptop. The Angels headed to Knox Technologies to tell Knox and Vivian the good news.

The company's grassy, tree-lined grounds were

about as opposite from Red Star's arid desert compound as you could get. An assistant steered the Angels to an outdoor cafeteria.

While Friday-casual employees hackey-sacked, lunched, or napped nearby, Vivian and Knox sat at a picnic table, waiting for the Angels' report.

As soon as the Angels gave them the lowdown, Knox gazed at the trio with admiration.

"Now I know why I hired you," he said. "You're the best."

Dylan couldn't help but blush at the compliment. Of course she knew they were the best. Hadn't the President called to say those very words just a couple of months ago? But something about the way Knox said it made her feel strangely gaga.

"We should celebrate our success," Knox added, getting to his feet.

Was it Dylan's imagination, or was he blushing just a little bit when he added, "Who's up for a night on the town?"

"Sorry," Natalie piped up. "Plans."

"Me, too," Alex said. "Special evening with Jason."

Knox turned and gazed at Dylan.

"And you?" he asked quietly.

"I'm . . . busy, too," Dylan said. "Sorry."

She'd almost choked on the words. In fact, she'd almost slipped and said she was free, she was available, she was up for anything.

Instead, she merely returned Knox's longing look and toed the party line. Angels don't date clients. Period.

Dylan didn't need to remind Natalie and Alex of this, of course. As soon as Knox had dragged his baby browns away from Dylan to confer with Vivian, Dylan's partners were all over her.

"Is there something going on between you and Knox?" Alex asked Dylan gently. There was no need to lower her voice or take her bud aside. She was speaking Finnish. And the odds that Knox or Vivian understood Finnish were at least 100,000 to 1.

Dylan felt her face go hot. Guilt stabbed her in the gut. But she tried to keep her cool as she answered Alex in perfect, accentless Finnish of her own.

"Of course not," she said.

"Good," Alex answered quickly, looking apologetic. *"I mean, I didn't think so."*

Natalie jumped in. In Finnish. *"It's just that client relationships are a classically bad idea."*

"I agree," Dylan declared, nodding vigorously.

"We just wouldn't want to see anyone we care about getting hurt," Alex said sympathetically.

Isn't that my whole way of life? Dylan asked herself, feeling her stomach clench. So why can't I shake this one off? Even as she thought this, half of her was back in Knox's kitchen, swimming in his brown eyes, luxuriating in his kisses. . . .

Dylan blinked hard and tried to focus on Knox and Vivian's conversation.

"So," Vivian said, making typing motions with her fingers. "Where is it?"

"The laptop?" Alex said. "Bosley's got it back at the agency. He's running a program—looking for evidence of Knox's software in the Red Star system."

Vivian's face went just a bit whiter than its normal ghostly pallor.

"I'd feel better if we were doing our own analysis," she said stiffly. "Surely Eric would be the best—"

"Our goal was to see if they'd stolen your software," Natalie interrupted, as gently as possible. "It would be unethical to give you full access to their system."

"As soon as we have proof, we'll let you know," Dylan said.

Knox nodded and smiled directly at Dylan.

"That makes sense," he said. "Certainly."

But Dylan could see Vivian gritting her teeth. She tapped her high-heeled foot on the ground impatiently.

Dylan took it all in. Lighten up, girl, she thought. Workaholism is such a drag.

CHAPTER

9

The long day of deprogramming was almost over. As his laptop hummed, Bosley stretched and changed from his tweedy sports coat into a velvet smoking jacket and ascot. He caught his reflection in the mirror over the juice bar. Looking good, Boy Angel, he thought to himself. Very hip.

He glanced at his watch. There was just enough time to whip up a little penne arrabbiata before he settled in for Reege. Yes!

Bosley poured himself a glass of Chianti and repaired to the kitchen. As he chopped and sliced, he didn't hear the laptop tell him that there was no evidence of Knox Technologies software in Red Star's database. He was just bringing the garlic and hot peppers to a sizzle when the doorbell rang.

"Hmmm," Bosley murmured, setting down his spatula and moseying into the main room. He opened the door to Vivian Wood—as he'd never seen Vivian Wood before.

She wore a shiny leather jumpsuit. Her dark brown hair—unleashed from its usual twist into a shaggy 'do—danced around her shoulders. Ms. Wood was definitely unbuttoned. She was practically unhinged!

"Trick or treat for Unicef?" Vivian said coyly.

"Very nice costume, young lady," Bosley replied, eyeing her skintight togs. He opened the door wider so Vivian could saunter in.

"Thanks," Vivian tossed over her shoulder. She leaned languidly against the back of the couch. "I came back because I forgot something."

Bosley walked over to his desk and began shuffling some papers.

"Well, I'm sure it's still here. I—*mmmggghfff.*"

That was the sound of Bosley being kissed by Vivian Wood. In fact, she was smooching the living daylights out of him, clutching his jowly face with her long, sharp nails and pressing her leather-clad body against his.

Finally, Bosley jerked his face away from Vivian's and gasped for oxygen.

"I forgot to thank you," Vivian said.

"Ms. Wood," Bosley protested, smoothing his smoking jacket huffily. "There are some lines I never cross."

"Lines have never stopped me . . . John," Vivian said. She circled Bosley slowly, like a cat toying with an injured mouse. "And it's Miss. It's Vivian."

"Miss Vivian," Bosley protested, "we're involved in a *professional*—"

"May I?"

Vivian was pointing to the open bottle of wine Bosley had left on the coffee table, next to his solitary, half-drunk glass.

"Forgive me," Bosley said quietly. "I'll get you a glass."

He scurried into the kitchenette. In his flustered state, he had to open four cabinets before he remembered where he kept the wineglasses. His mind was reeling. Think of the possibilities. Think of the ethical dilemma. Think of the spots on this wineglass! Oh, the gaucheness!

Bosley gave the glass a quick polish as Vivian called from the other room, "I've never known a man like you."

"Know me?" Bosley said, returning to the main room. "You can't. *We* can't."

He picked up the bottle of Chianti and poured Vivian a glass, just as she seemed to see the point of his argument. She hung her head for a moment, then said, "You're right, of course. I should go."

"Yes," Bosley said, though he'd hoped she'd put up a bit more of a fight than *that*. "Yes, of course you must. I'm glad you see the wisdom."

With a last lingering, sultry squint, Vivian stalked out of the agency. But for a whiff of Poison perfume in the air, she might never have been there at all.

Bosley was left clutching her glass of untouched wine. He lifted it in a melancholy toast.

"To what might have been," he sighed. Then he took a deep swig.

October 21, 8:38 P.M.
Location: Eric Knox's house, Laurel Canyon
Status: Client no more

After the sun set, Dylan somehow found herself at Knox's round glass mansion. The place was all lit up from the inside. To Dylan, it looked like a beacon.

She took a deep breath, hurried up Knox's walk, and rang the bell. Knox answered the door, looking sleepy. But when he saw Dylan, his face broke into a sweet smile.

"Hi," Dylan said.

"Hi."

The silence between them thrummed with tension.

"So . . ." Dylan said, "case closed, right?"

Knox grinned. In an instant, they were kissing, kissing passionately, barely breathing. Finally, they came up for air, laughing. And then they were kissing some more as they stumbled backward.

Knox extricated himself from their embrace for a moment and gazed at Dylan tenderly. She kicked off her boots.

With a flick of his wrist, Knox swung the front door closed.

October 21, 8:38 P.M.
Location: Roger Corwin's penthouse. The Japanese lagoon
Status: A moment of repose

Roger Corwin had had a satisfying day. He'd presided over a hostile takeover of yet another Internet start-up. Then, for kicks, he'd fired a malcontent Red Star manager.

"That'll be the last time that fella puts a picture of his wife and kids up in one of *my* cubicles," Corwin cackled.

Now he had the evening to himself. He just wanted to relax with a snifter of brandy and some pirated cable TV in his steamy, soothing lagoon.

Aaaaah . . .

Ah! What's this?

Hearing footsteps on the moist rock pathway behind him, Corwin twisted in his chair. There he saw one of his many staff members—his go-to man when it came to anything seedy, sordid, or violent. Man, that skinny, black-haired guy creeped him out with those icy, blue eyes.

Corwin scowled in annoyance and said, "I wasn't expecting—*urfffggggh.*"

A minute later the Thin Man wiped a few speckles of blood off his cane and gazed at Corwin's body. The satellite magnate was slumped in his bamboo recliner. A blunt wound on his forehead was oozing blood. A growing cloud of red swirled in the lagoon's steamy waters.

The brandy snifter fell from Corwin's limp hand and shattered with a weak, tinkling noise.

Then, his face as stony as always, the Thin Man left the building.

* * *

October 21, 8:38 P.M.
Location: Jack's, a sidewalk café
Status: Having the Talk

Everything was perfect. Jason Gibbons was gazing at his raven-haired sweetie across a cozy table at their favorite outdoor eatery. The waitress had just served the first course when a guitarist strolled up to the table, plucking a soothing melody.

She moved to speak, but Jason held up his hand.

"No," he protested. "I know you have something to say, but I have something to say first."

He took a deep breath, flicked aside an errant strand of his brown hair and said, "I've been thinking a lot about you. And me. And us. And I know we have these crazy lives, but I can't help it. I love you. And I want to be with you and protect you for the rest of my life. I guess what I'm trying to say is . . . will you marry me?"

Jason reached for his beloved's hand. Their fingertips were just touching—an electric, thrilling touch—when a loud crack sounded in the distance. Suddenly the woman to whom Jason had just pledged his love shuddered violently. Her chest exploded in a spray of blood and gore. She pitched forward, landing face-down in the chopped salad.

She was dead.

Jason gasped in disbelief while diners at nearby tables screamed, dropped their panini, upended their chairs, and fled. Tears sprang to Jason's baby browns. He leaped to his feet. His every bicep and pectoral was flexed. He was in shock. And then he was enraged.

"Oh, baby . . . no! God, no!" Jason screamed, staring at the cascade of glossy black hair on the tablecloth, gaping at the blood that spattered his hands and his tight white T-shirt. Suddenly a realization dawned on him. His face contorted in horror.

"Damn you, Salazar," he yelled, tears streaming down his face. He gazed into the heavens and shook his fist. *"Damn you, Salazar!"*

"Cut!"

Jason grinned and turned to the director of *L.A. Underwater*.

"Was that over the top?" he asked as the raven-haired woman—a stuntwoman—got up from the table. "That felt over the top."

October 21, 8:38 P.M.
Location: Jason Gibbons's trailer, Pacific Pictures
    studio lot
Weapon: The truth—even if it hurts

Meanwhile, Jason's real-life raven-haired love was laboring over a "Sensual Dinner for Two," as featured in the September issue of *Gourmet* magazine.

She'd decorated Jason's Airstream trailer with a tasteful bouquet of orchids, just like in the picture in *Gourmet*. And she'd lit vanilla-scented votive candles all over the trailer, just like in the picture in *Gourmet*. She had pulled a delicate chocolate soufflé out of the

CHARLIE'S ANGELS

Dylan Sanders
Always finds the good in people

Natalie Cook
Optimistic, shy, and deceptively brilliant

Alex Munday
Sophisticated and unstoppable

At the Charles Townsend Agency, the Angels' home away from home

Under cover at Roger Corwin's penthouse party

A Chinatown alley . . .

a formidable
opponent, the
Thin Man . . .

and the captive:
Eric Knox

L.A. County Freeway:
Dash for Cash—and
criminals

A disguise for
every situation

Visiting Red
Star Systems
headquarters

For Dylan, a dinner invitation à la Eric Knox

For Alex and Jason, one more good-bye

For Natalie, a dream date with Pete

The agency's been blown up and Bosley is missing—now the Angels are on their own

From their command post Eric Knox and Vivian Wood plot to get rid of the Angels

Natalie drops into fighting stance, ready for anything

Natalie frees Bosley from his bachelor cell

ANGELS FOREVER

oven and was garnishing a roast with cherry peppers and rosemary sprigs, just like in the . . . well, you get the idea.

The roast, it must be admitted, was a bit on the charred side. And the rosemary sprigs weren't staying in place. Alex sighed and distracted herself by rehearsing her speech to Jason.

"How was your day?" she said, posing the question to the air. "Great, and you know how superheroes have secret identities . . ."

Alex rolled her eyes. Terrible. And what was up with these rosemary sprigs? How did those *Gourmet* people get them to stick so cunningly out of the roast? Hers were just flopping over limply.

"Grrrrr," Alex fumed. She glanced around the apartment in frustration. Ah-ha! There was a prop AK-47 semiautomatic sitting in the corner.

Once upon a time, Alex had attended Navy SEAL boot camp, just for kicks. So, of course, she knew how to field-strip one of these guns in under thirty seconds. Alex pounced on the weapon. She broke it quickly and neatly into fifteen components, one of which was a skewerlike trigger-lock mechanism.

Alex gripped the sharp instrument and poked a series of holes in the roast. Then she reassembled the gun in 28.4 seconds—a new record.

Alex shoved the rosemary sprigs into the meat. They stuck, perkily, just like the picture in *Gourmet*.

She tried out another way to tell Jason what she did. "I'm one third of an elite crime-fighting team backed by an anonymous millionaire. Perfect!" Alex pronounced.

Ki-chang.

The perfect roast exploded into a thousand meaty clumps.

Alex spun around in shock. The fact registered in her gut before she could comprehend it with her mind—a single bullet had just pierced the trailer's wall and blown her roast to smithereens.

Before she could dive for cover, bullets began pouring into her boyfriend's trailer at the speed of sound, ripping into the walls as if they were made of paper.

Alex's instincts took over.

She leaped through the air, catching the upper cabinets with her fingertips.

With one power crunch of her abs, Alex swung her legs upward, pressing her entire body against the ceiling. She hovered there, in permanent pull-up mode, while bullets tore through every inch of the airspace beneath her.

Only her strength would save her life.

Alex gritted her teeth and felt her triceps begin to tremble. Feathers from the duvet on Jason's bed floated past her nose. She was vaguely aware of the refrigerator cracking open like Humpty Dumpty. The television exploded in mid-commercial. And oh! Her soufflé! Alex craned her neck to peek at her luscious, fragile dessert. Miraculously, the soufflé hadn't been hit and was still standing, as puffy and luscious as ever.

But still, the bullets kept on coming.

Only when the entire length of the trailer had been reduced to Swiss cheese did the shots dwindle, then stop.

Alex took another peek at her soufflé. It was still up, still beautiful!

She was just about to drop to the floor when a last spattering of bullets pumped through the trailer.

Hisssssss.

That would be the sound of a soufflé falling.

"Rrrrrrr!"

And that would be the sound of one very enraged amateur chef.

Alex heard an engine rev outside. She dropped to the floor and ran to peer out the shattered window. A black Humvee with deeply tinted windows was peeling out of the studio lot.

Alex dashed to the door and threw it open. It fell off in her hand, tumbling to the ground with a pathetic crunch. Alex leaped over the door remnants and began to run after the Humvee. So what if she was barefoot and shaken? So what if the shooter was driving away at 40 mph? That jerk ruined my dinner! Alex thought. Only one thing could stop her now.

"Hey!"

"Jason!" Alex cried. There was her very own b.f., sauntering to his trailer. Alex looked at his white T-shirt and saw red. Correction—she saw blood. Jason was covered with blood!

"My God," she cried. "You're hit! You're—"

"Fine," Jason interrupted with a flirty smile. "I'm fine. I mean the squibs hurt a bit when they pop, but I'm okay."

He swiped some red stuff off his shirt and put his finger to her lips. She tasted cherry.

"Oh," Alex said, still shaking. "Heh. Heh-heh."

"Why are you acting so weird?" Jason said, squinting at her.

"Jason . . ." Alex began. She flicked a glass shard off her shoulder and then looked her hunkola right in the eyes. "I haven't been honest with you. The thing is, I'm not a bikini waxer."

Jason looked confused. And a little angry? Or maybe that was his grief-stricken face. Alex could never tell with actors. Finally he settled on an expression that was definitely mild disappointment.

"Bummer," Jason said, wide-eyed. "That was kind of a turn-on."

October 21, 8:38 P.M.
Location: A nondescript TV studio in Hollywood
Status: A second chance

Waiting for Pete at this strange, unmarked building, Natalie was deep into predate jitters. Especially since the sweetie hadn't told her what he had planned when they'd talked on the phone earlier.

A throng of hipsters flowed into the building. Everyone seemed to be wearing cool, retro threads, body glitter, Manolos, the works. Finally, Natalie spotted Pete. Hello! Out of his bartender togs, Pete was even cuter.

"Hey, Pete!" Natalie called, jogging up to him.

"Hi," he said, grinning at Natalie with bald-faced admiration. "You want your ticket?" he asked, waving it in front of her face with a sweet grin.

"Are you kidding?" Natalie said, swiping the ticket out of his hand playfully. "Thanks for the second chance."

"That's okay," Pete said. "I really, really wanted to see you again."

Natalie could feel her face flush. Gushy vibes and embarrassment coursed through her. The only thing to do was look for a distraction. She gestured toward the stream of satin-clad Beautiful People.

"So, what is this?" she asked Pete.

"I really can't say," he said, opening the door for Natalie. "Except that I wanted tonight to be great, so I got tickets for something special."

Then they walked, literally, into Natalie's dream. *Soul Train.*

Everything was there: the mirrored disco balls; the fabulous sound system; and of course a sweating, gyrating crowd of the best dancers in the area, with cameramen dodging and weaving among them.

Natalie glanced down at her skin-tight black pants, her one-shouldered red tank, and her pointy-toed stiletto heels. She breathed a thank-you to the disco gods for inspiring her to go Halstonesque tonight. Then she stared, open-mouthed and enraptured, at the scene.

"I hope you like to dance," Pete yelled over the throbbing music.

"Are you kidding?" Natalie gushed. "I love to dance!"

But she couldn't seem to move her feet. It was all too . . . perfect.

Scratch that. It was just about to get better.

"Hey," said a raspy voice behind Natalie.

She turned around to face two burly, bouncer types in black *Soul Train* T-shirts.

"You want to dance on the stage?" one of them asked.

"Us?" Pete squeaked. He looked at Natalie. Natalie looked at him. Then they both looked at the bouncers and yelled, "Yeah!"

"Uh, sorry," said the talkative bouncer. "The stage is for the lady."

Pete's face fell.

"Okay," he said.

Natalie bit her lip and said, "Well, that's okay, then. Don't worry about it. I'll find a spot on the floor."

The bouncers shrugged and started to lumber away.

Pete ran after them and grabbed their meaty shoulders.

"Wait!" he said to Natalie. "Wait a second. That's *Soul Train*'s highest honor. I'm not going to let you not go up there. Seriously, she'll go, guys. Really."

"Really?" Natalie asked.

Pete gazed at his date softly and said, "Seriously. I'll see you later."

Then he drifted into the crowd and the bouncers led Natalie onto the *Soul Train* stage.

Natalie stood stock-still for a moment. She couldn't believe this was happening to her.

But in an instant she started to dance.

She didn't just groove—swing her hips, roll her head, shimmy her shoulders. No, Natalie incorporated every element of her fantasies into her dance. She was kick-boxing and swimming and shaking her hips and Rollerblading. She was a postmodern goddess. It was Natalie's world. The rest of the *Soul Train* hipsters just lived there.

Which must have been why some of them didn't quite get Natalie's thing. What they saw were moves that no one had done in years. Titters began to fill the room. They were making fun of the oblivious Natalie.

All of them, that is, except Pete.

He was gazing at his date with pure admiration. He sidled up to one of the bouncers and slapped him on the shoulder.

"Isn't she *amazing?*" he enthused over the music. "She's pretty great, huh? My name's Pete, by the way. It's the first time we've been out, you know."

Pete gave the bouncer's shoulder a happy, friendly squeeze.

"I think things are going pretty well," he yelled. "Wow, you guys are in really good shape."

The bouncer rolled his eyes at Pete and walked away. But Pete couldn't move. He was riveted by the lovely Natalie, by the way she flailed her arms over her head in concentric circles, the way she jumped in place like Gwen Stefani on twenty cups of coffee.

She was divine. Pete was smitten. And the crowd was now, too, won over by Natalie's enthusiasm.

Finally, the song ended and Natalie bounded off the stage to the spot where Pete was waiting.

"Incredible," he intoned. "You were great."

"Really?" Natalie gushed. She would have blushed if her face wasn't already red and sweaty. She couldn't get her hips to stop shimmying back and forth. She shook her hair out and yelled, "I'm having so much fun. This is so exciting!"

As she danced around Pete, she caught a glimpse of herself in one of the many mirrors that surrounded the dance floor. She was a mess—her hair mussed, her clothes in disarray. She leaned close to Pete and yelled, "I think I'll go freshen up."

Natalie floated out of the studio and headed into the bathroom. When she glanced into the mirror, she had a totally goofy smile on her face.

She leaned over a sink and splashed a little cold water on her cheeks. As she straightened up, she said dreamily, "Oh, I could just die."

That's when she saw the face in the mirror. A glowering, dirt-smudged, man's face hovering right behind hers. He'd come out of nowhere. And so did that chain.

The man flipped the nunchuk over Natalie's neck with a vicious grunt.

"Accccchh," Natalie gurgled. She felt her feet leave the floor and her throat close like a trap. She pulled her knees to her chest, found the edge of the sink with her toes and pushed, doing a back flip over the creep's shoulder and whipping her neck out of the nunchuk.

Natalie took a gulp of air as she sideswiped the attacker's head with the back of her elbow. He spun around and Natalie used the momentum to dig her knee into his stomach.

He threw a left hook and connected with Natalie's mouth—totally ruining her lipstick. Natalie growled in anger and delivered a series of stunning punches to the guy's head. Then she aimed a round kick at his neck and shoved her heel into his windpipe, pinning him to the wall.

"Who do you work for?" she barked.

The guy made an angry, choking noise and swiped at Natalie's ankle. But she wasn't budging. In fact, she pressed harder.

"Speak now or never again," she threatened.

"Woo . . . woo . . . ," the man rasped.

"Stop crying and tell me the name!" Natalie demanded.

"Wood," he finally gasped. "Vivian Wood."

Natalie blinked hard and dropped her foot from the man's neck. Before he could run away, she rammed her palm into his sternum and shoved him back against the wall. Just then a cell phone rang.

It was his.

Natalie glared at the guy and fished around in the

pocket of his leather jacket. She yanked the phone out and used her thumb to flip it open. Then she jammed it against his ear.

"Hello?" he quavered.

Natalie leaned in to listen. She instantly recognized Vivian's chilly voice.

"Is she dead?" Vivian demanded.

"Say yes," Natalie mouthed, digging her knuckles into the guy's chest. He winced and said, "Yes."

Natalie clicked off the cell phone and gave the guy one more shattering blow to the jaw, knocking him out cold. Then she pulled a pair of handcuffs out of her evening bag—because an Angel never leaves home without 'em—and cuffed the thug's limp body to a bathroom stall.

Natalie slumped against the sinks for a moment. Near-death experiences were such a buzzkill.

And her buzz-source had probably bailed. She'd been gone for, like, fifteen minutes!

Natalie rushed back into the studio and gazed wistfully at Pete, who was looking at the door, waiting for her.

"I'm so sorry," she whispered when she reached him, "but I have to go. I can't explain."

Pete's face fell and Natalie bit her lip. She grabbed a pen out of her bag and wrote her digits on Pete's palm.

"This is my cell phone number," she said. "Please call me tomorrow. Please. I'm sorry."

Natalie started out of the studio, but the image of Pete's sad, sweet face was blocking her vision.

So she spun around. She stalked back to her date and she laid a kiss on his lips—a quick, totally intense, really wonderful kiss. When she pulled away, Pete looked happily dazed. She was feeling a little woozy herself.

She flashed one final smile at her new sweetie and dashed out of the building.

CHAPTER

10

October 21, 9:46 P.M.
Location: Outside the *Soul Train* studio
Status: Dissed, disheveled, and disturbed

As soon as she hit the sidewalk, the goofy, lovesick smile vanished from Natalie's lips. If Vivian was out to kill one Angel, she must be out for all three. But why?

The answer came to Natalie like a punch in the gut. Vivian must be on Corwin's team. She was getting them out of the way so that this time Corwin could finish Knox off.

Natalie pulled out her cell phone as she pushed her way through a throng of dancers. She speed-dialed Dylan's cell. After four rings, her g.f. answered, sounding sleepy.

"Dyl, it's Nat," Natalie said urgently. "Listen, Vivian Wood is the bad guy. She's a paid assassin and a major pain in the butt. And on my date night, too! Anyway, we have to warn Knox."

* * *

October 21, 9:47 P.M.
Location: Eric Knox's bedroom
Wardrobe: Not much

Dylan was sitting up in Knox's bed. She'd woken up to the bleeping of her cell phone and the bittersweet realization that she was wearing little besides her underwear.

Still half-asleep, she tried to comprehend Natalie's frantic words. Vivian—bad guy. Gotta warn Knox. Knox!

"I'm at Knox's house right now," Dylan blurted.

"You are?" Natalie blurted right back.

Uh-oh. Had Dylan said that out loud? She sighed and said wearily, "Call Alex. I'll meet you at the agency."

"Dylan . . ." Natalie said. Her voice was prickly with disappointment. Dylan couldn't hack it. She pretended not to hear and hung up.

She grabbed the top sheet off of Knox's bed and wrapped it around herself. The thought of Knox in danger made her break into a run.

But when she reached the living area, there he was, safe. He was standing in front of the huge, floor-to-ceiling windows that overlooked the canyon.

Knox sipped a drink as he gazed into the night. He looked contented. Candles flickered around the room and jazz was piping softly out of the stereo.

"Get back from the windows," Dylan said. Her voice was still a little hoarse from her nap. "It's not safe."

Knox turned and took in Dylan with a blissed-out smile. Her bare shoulders peeked out of the sheet. Her red hair was tousled and tangled.

"It's not safe anywhere," he said with a low laugh. "Safety is an illusion of the modern world."

Dylan took a few more steps toward Knox and then stopped. She spotted something on the coffee table: a second drink. And it wasn't hers.

"Who else is here?" Dylan said, feeling a catch in her throat.

"It's only me."

The voice crept up the back of Dylan's neck like a splash of ice water—Vivian Wood. Dylan turned to see the woman herself whip around in a swivel chair by the fireplace. Dylan's eyes widened. Vivian was wearing a tight black sleeveless dress that revealed arms used to pumping serious iron. Vivian held an open cell phone in her hand.

"Working under cover?" Vivian said, eyeing Dylan and the sheet.

Dylan sneered and said, "We're a full-service agency."

"I can see by your gown that you're unarmed," Vivian reproached Dylan. "Some maniac could just stroll in here and blow you both away."

Dylan tried hard not to scowl. Okay, Vivian, she thought. You've made your point, loud and clear. One false move, and we're both dead.

Knox didn't have a clue. He plopped onto the couch, grabbed a magazine and said, "Vivian, you're obsessed. All work and no play."

Vivian ignored Knox and put her phone back to her ear.

"I just need to tie up some loose ends," she said.

If Knox hadn't been there, Dylan might have made a move—might have done *something*. But she couldn't endanger him. She huffed in frustration. This witch had Dylan right where she wanted her. There was nothing she could do except flop onto the couch next to Knox.

Vivian spoke into the phone.

"I'm back. . . . Uh-huh, that's one. Yes, I *know* what Swiss cheese looks like . . ."

Dylan didn't know exactly what Vivian was referring to, but she felt a chill skitter up her spine. She only felt chillier when Vivian's face broke into an evil grin.

"Oh, poor Miss Mouse caught inside," Vivian crooned sarcastically.

She glanced at Dylan.

"I'll be a second," she whispered, and pointed to a game of Scrabble that happened to be lying open on the coffee table. "Scrabble, you two?"

Perfect.

Dylan faked a yawn. Then she began to futz idly with the Scrabble tiles. Casually, she slid an *E* onto a free square. Then an *N*. Then another *E*.

In a second she nudged Knox and pointed at the Scrabble board. Her tiles formed a word now: *ENEMY.* Dylan gestured slightly toward Vivian.

Knox glanced at the board and his face lit up.

"Good word!" he declared. "Ten points *and* a double letter on *Y.*"

Dylan shook her head at Knox and frowned. Then she gestured again toward Vivian, who was saying, "Yes, I just heard. And she was the *smart* one."

Knox's face turned cryptic. He squinted at Dylan for a long moment. Then he gave her a quick kiss and said, "I know."

Dylan blinked, not comprehending.

Knox turned to her with a sardonic little smile, and Dylan felt the breath being sucked from her lungs. What was happening here?

In a word: betrayal.

Vivian snapped her phone closed and addressed Dylan. "Sad news," she said brightly. "Your girlfriends are dead."

Vivian reached into her boxy black purse and pulled out a snub-nosed gun. Dylan sized it up—a nine-millimeter Remington.

The silver muzzle glinted in the candlelight. Vivian laid the revolver, suggestively, on the coffee table.

Dylan leaped to her feet. She felt her stomach roil with confusion.

"And what about Corwin?" Vivian said, addressing someone behind Dylan. Dylan spun around. The Thin Man! Somehow he'd escaped death in the car crash at the bridge. He glared at Dylan with those pale eyes and merely nodded.

When Dylan spun back to face Vivian, she found herself staring down the glittering muzzle of Vivian's gun.

Knox gave Dylan a dismissive sneer and stepped over to Vivian's side, humming along with the jazz piping out of the speakers. Then he spoke. He spoke with a new voice, in fact. It was deeper and more confident than the one Dylan had come to know. Correction: the voice Dylan had *thought* she'd known.

"Let me get this straight," he spat. "You're a woman *and* a detective, and you had no idea this was gonna happen?"

Vivian stepped close to Knox and planted a sultry kiss on the back of his neck.

"*I* knew," she purred. "And I know what's going to happen next."

Knox took the gun from Vivian and aimed it at Dylan himself.

"All the Angels will go to heaven," Vivian continued in a chilling singsong.

"What about Bosley?" Dylan demanded.

"Bosley," Vivian said with a dry laugh, "is coming with us to hell."

Dylan felt a stab in her stomach, but she didn't let on. Her mind was whirring as all the pieces fell instantly into place.

"Corwin had nothing to do with this," she murmured.

Knox nodded.

"Your kidnapping was a hoax," Dylan said.

Knox nodded again, a self-satisfied smile playing around the corners of his mouth.

"And Red Star," Dylan said, feeling nauseous, "it was all a setup?"

Knox shrugged happily. Dylan felt the hairs on her neck bristle. She was dealing with a psychopath here.

She'd been *making out* with a psychopath here. All of a sudden, a realization hit her like a medicine ball to the stomach.

"It's Charlie," she whispered. "You're after Charlie. Why?"

Knox smiled grimly.

"They say that in death," Knox said creepily, "all life's questions are answered."

Dylan tensed, feeling every muscle in her body prepare for action.

Knox's eyes widened and his smile turned into a quivery leer.

"Let me know if that's true," he said.

He squeezed the trigger.

The plate glass window exploded as Dylan crashed through it. She flailed and fell, headfirst, into the black night.

CHAPTER

11

October 21, 10:13 P.M.
Location: Home of Eric Knox
Device: Instant replay

Knox pointed the gun at Dylan.

"They say that in death," he said, "all life's questions are answered. Let me know if that's true."

Dylan spied the vein throbbing in Knox's temple and the slight, pre-explosion kick of the revolver. She saw it coming when . . .

Knox squeezed the trigger.

Instinctively, Dylan twisted to the left, hurling herself blindly out of the way.

She felt a rush of heat cross her left shoulder. She heard glass exploding. Her feet skidded out from beneath her. And then she was falling, falling into blackness. Her arms were outstretched, grabbing for anything that might save her.

Hazily Dylan became conscious of a few key things.

1) She was not dead.
2) She was not hit. The bullet must have skimmed

within a centimeter of her, shattering the window instead of her own heart.

3) She was wearing nothing but a blue satin bikini and matching bra.

4) One corner of Knox's bedsheet was snagged on a shard of broken glass jutting out of the window frame. She was clutching the other end with both fists. The only thing between Dylan and an 80-foot plummet was this stretch of 500-thread count Egyptian cotton.

For a moment Dylan simply clung to the sheet, trying to catch her breath as she swung in midair. Around her, the night was chilly and eerily quiet.

So that's what near-death feels like, she thought. Then she shook her head to chase the thought away.

She wasn't out of the woods yet.

Dylan gazed above her head. The window was about twelve feet away. As delicately as she could, she began to climb the sheet, hand over hand.

She'd made it halfway when she heard it.

Zip.

That was the sound of a very expensive bedsheet beginning to tear. Dylan froze and squeezed her eyes shut.

The rip stopped.

She gulped some oxygen and began to climb again.

Ziiippp.

The sheet tore some more. Dylan could see the fabric opening like a spiteful, laughing mouth.

ZIPPPPPP.

"Damn," Dylan said.

Then the sheet split in two and she went into a free fall.

"Ooof," she grunted, hitting the steep cliffside with a thud. Before she could grab a root, a rock, or anything, she was somersaulting down the mountain.

As she fell, she cursed Knox. With every bump, scrape, roll, and tumble, she screamed out her rage. She'd been duped by yet another guy. And this time, it might get her killed!

When Dylan finally skidded to a halt, her bare arms and legs had been rubbed raw by the mountainside. But she hopped to her feet almost immediately.

She had work to do.

She stalked over to a nearby bungalow. She could see the blue glow of a television through the sliding screen doors of a basement rec room. When she peered inside, she almost groaned. Sitting in front of the TV were two boys. Two *little* boys, about eight years old. They were playing Virtua Fighter on a Playstation 2.

Dylan looked down at her bod. Not only was she scarred and bruised, her undies were in tatters.

"On top of everything else," she muttered, "I have to corrupt the youth of America to get out of this fix?"

As she worked up the courage to knock on the door, she caught a snippet of the kids' conversation.

"So, what did it look like?" one kid asked.

"I dunno," said his friend, jamming his phaser button. "It was all like, cool and stuff."

The other kid stared at his bud and shook his head. "Liar," he pronounced. "You've never *seen* a boobie."

Oh, boy, Dylan thought.

"Have, too," retorted the other kid.

"Have not!"

"I've seen lotsa boobies."

"Nuh-uh."

"Yuh-huh."

"Nuh-uh!"

"Yuh-huh!"

"Um, hi there." The boys whipped around and spotted Dylan. She stood outside the screen door, awkwardly covering what was left of her bra and panties with an inflatable pool dragon.

Dylan cringed as the boys' mouths dropped to their chests and their eyes bugged out.

"A little help?" she begged.

October 21, 11:49 P.M.
Location: The Townsend Agency parking lot
Wardrobe: Something borrowed, something blue

Alex was just arriving at the agency when Natalie roared up in her Ferrari. She was stripping her gears she was so angry. She screeched to a halt and jumped out of the car.

"Where's Dylan?" Alex said, gazing down the almost-deserted street.

Putt-putt-putt-putt.

Natalie and Alex whirled around. There was Dylan

astride a small, slow-moving dirt bike. Her knees were skinned, and her hair literally looked like a bird's nest—twigs, leaves, and all. She was wearing baggy blue gym shorts, an oversized WWF T-shirt and a bunch of Pokémon Band-Aids.

Dylan crawled off the bike painfully. She looked at her partners who, naturally, were gaping at her outfit.

"Don't ask," Dylan murmured.

"Is Knox okay?" Alex asked.

"Oh, he's great," Dylan spat, stalking up the walk toward the agency. "He's the bad guy. The kidnapping was a setup. He's behind the whole thing."

"What?" Natalie blurted, stumbling after Dylan. "Why?"

"He wasn't exactly forthcoming when he shot me out the window," Dylan said angrily. She headed to the agency door.

But before she could get there, the Charles Townsend Agency exploded.

Fireballs rippled out of the windows and blew the door off its hinges. The blast's force lifted the Angels off their feet and hurled them backward—directly into the windshield of Alex's Mercedes. In a word—crunch.

A minute or so later, Dylan slowly sat up on the car's hood. She felt her already sore body creak and groan.

She checked out her buds. Like her, they were stunned and wincing, but they were okay.

The same could not be said for the agency, the

homey little building where they'd spent so many hours; the safe haven that had always been there for them, no matter what bombs, bullets, or man-eating sharks crossed their paths.

All that was going up in flames.

Fire bulged out of the windows. The building seemed to crumble inside the hot, chemical-fueled blaze.

The three watched their agency burn, hypnotized, until Natalie gasped.

"Oh my God. Bosley!" she cried.

"He's safe," Dylan cut in. "Knox already has him."

"Let me put this together," Alex said, sliding off the hood of her formerly fabulous car and landing, shakily, on her feet. "You're saying Bosley is with the man who just tried to kill us? How does that make him safe?"

Dylan held up her hand and said, "He's going to keep Bosley alive until he kills Charlie."

"Oh, that's kind of good, right?" Natalie offered hopefully.

"Kills Charlie," Alex said. She planted her fists on her hips and glared. "Jeez, Dylan . . ."

"Why are you throwing this like it's all my fault?" Dylan demanded.

"Well, you were kinda fooling around with the bad guy," Natalie pointed out gently.

"What!" Alex yelled, glaring some more.

Dylan couldn't speak. Nat was so right, but Dylan's pride wouldn't let her admit it. Instead, she locked eyes with her partners and said in low and lethal tones, "Look. I don't know what his plan is yet. But I know we can stop him."

"How, Dylan?" Alex cried. "We don't have Charlie. We don't have Bosley. We don't have an agency."

Natalie had been slumped against the bumper of the car, watching in disgust as her fellow Angels ripped into each other. Now she'd had enough.

"You're right, okay?" she exclaimed, jumping between her buds. "You're completely right. We don't have anything—except one another. But that's all we've ever needed before."

There was a long silence, filled only with the angry crackling of the fire. Then Alex's teeth unclenched. She shot Dylan a rueful look and said quietly, "Okay, let's figure this out."

October 22, 4:02 A.M.
Location: Charles Townsend Detective Agency
Status: Demoralized

The firefighters had just left. The Angels found themselves at the threshold of their office. They were silent—dumbstruck actually, their throats clogged with smoke and soot and raw emotion.

Without speaking, the Angels picked their way around charred furniture and dripping bookshelves. Over their heads, they saw burned timbers. The room was filled with a melancholy drip, drip, dripping.

"If Knox thinks we're all dead," Dylan wondered, "why did he blow up the agency?"

"He must have wanted to erase any connection between us and Knox Technologies," Alex said, sitting on the arm of one of the ruined couches. "All we know for sure is that Knox wanted us to break into Red Star."

Natalie cringed as she recalled wiring into Red Star's mainframe.

"He used us to tap into Red Star's system," she said, "and gain control of the company's global positioning satellites."

"And, of course, he's got the key to audio DNA," Alex mused. Then she gasped, remembering that the first time Vivian Wood had come to the office, she'd gone to so much trouble to cross the room and place her purse right next to Charlie's speakerphone.

"Vivian must have taped Charlie's voice!" she exclaimed. "With his software, Knox could match Charlie's voice on the phone—"

"And use Red Star's satellite to track him," Natalie finished.

"But why would Knox go to all this trouble to find Charlie?" Alex wondered.

Dylan squeezed her eyes shut. You know him best, she thought. Think!

Suddenly a scene flashed into her memory. That snapshot of Knox's father. He had been with another man—a blurred, mysterious fellow.

"My father's best friend," Knox had said. "He turned on him."

The blurry guy—was he Charlie?

Dylan's eyes flew open.

"Why go to all this trouble?" she repeated. "Because I'm betting Knox thinks Charlie killed his father."

The Angels looked at one another, each a little paler than she'd been a moment ago.

"If Knox can intercept Charlie when he uses his cell phone . . ." Natalie began.

"Knox will be able to pinpoint Charlie's exact location," Dylan finished.

"But," Natalie said, "he has to get Charlie on the phone to start the trace."

"And no one knows how to reach him," Alex said urgently. She leaped to her feet in alarm. "The only person Charlie calls directly is—"

"Bosley," Dylan said darkly.

October 22, Dawn
Location: A locked room, somewhere near the ocean
Wardrobe: Basic hostage wear

Bosley had always thought being held hostage would have more . . . glamour. He'd pictured himself in a prison, sunken-cheeked and wan, yet also palely beautiful. And brave. Yes, even noble. He'd never give in. He'd *never* talk, no matter what they did to him!

The thing is, nobody cared what Bosley had to say. His jailer, that blue-eyed skinny guy, had just ignored Bosley's chatter when he came into the bare-bones, decrepit cell to dump his food tray the night before.

Bosley had been too traumatized to eat, of course. Well, except for the chocolate pudding. That pudding had been just to die for.

But when the pudding couldn't distract Bosley, his demons took over. He raced to his tiny, barred window and screamed, "HEEEELLLPPPP," until he was hoarse.

He found himself pacing the room like a tiger in a cage. Okay, more like a housecat in a locked beachside condo.

But still! He was dying for human contact. He was so desperate that he found himself chatting up a cheeping black-and-yellow bird that perched on his windowsill.

Then, in spurts of energy, Bosley hatched plans to save himself. He yanked all the stuffing out of his smelly cot mattress and fashioned it into a Bos-shaped lump under his bedsheet. Then he took the other sheet and tore it into strips. With those, he fashioned a rope and tied it to a window bar. Somehow, some way, he'd squeeze out and climb down . . . Oh.

Bosley had just realized he was in a cliffside fortress, one hundred feet above a rocky beach. His rope was an impotent four feet long. He collapsed with a sob onto the floor.

His feathered friend cheeped sympathetically.

In a stupor, Bosley pulled out the one bit of amusement the Thin Man had allowed him—a baseball and mitt. Still sprawled on the floor, he began tossing the ball against the wall, catching it as it thwacked back toward him.

Toss. *Thwack.*

Toss. *Thwack.*

Toss. *Bzzzzzttt.*

"Oooooowwww!"

The ball had made an odd bounce and slammed into Bosley's jaw with a crack. An oddly electronic crack.

Bosley stuck his finger into his mouth and fingered his sore tooth. And that's when something fell into his palm.

Bosley peered at the object in his hand and smiled. At last, at last—a break. Or to be more specific—a molar mic.

October 22, Dawn

Location: The remains of the Charles Townsend Detective Agency

Status: Disheveled and desperate

The Angels' mission was clear, simple even. It also seemed impossible. They had to find Bosley before Charlie called Bosley. And, as they all knew, that call would arrive at 9 A.M. on the dot.

Clues. They needed clues. They rushed over to Bosley's desk, which had been overturned by the fire-fighters' hoses. With a great heave, the Angels righted it and watched black water pour out of the drawers. Then they began sifting through Bosley's things—a melted plastic Rolodex, singed files, a decimated computer.

Natalie faltered for a moment, slumping over. She was exhausted. She was overwhelmed.

"Any sign of the laptop?" Dylan asked.

"Knox must have grabbed it when they took Bosley," Natalie said.

Alex stopped sifting through a file drawer and announced, "We should check his place for leads."

Dylan began stalking to the door.

"Let's move," she grunted.

Then Dylan heard something.

It was a faint murmuring, somewhere near a corner of the office.

"Angels?"

She looked up sharply. Was that her imagination? She glanced at Natalie and Dylan. They were gazing at the corner, too.

Natalie gasped in disbelief.

"I don't know if you can hear me," the voice said.

All at once, the Angels rushed to the corner, seeking out the muffled speaker.

Dylan pointed to a fallen bookcase. Together they shoved it aside to discover a half-crushed radio receiver. It crackled and the voice sounded again.

"I don't know if this thing is even working," it said.

"Bosley?" Natalie cried.

"I know you can't answer," Bosley said, "but I really hope you can hear this."

The Angels gaped at one another. Hope glinted in their eyes for the first time in hours.

"Any way to trace him?" Dylan said.

"Even if we had our equipment," Alex said, "he'd have to be within twenty miles."

"Come on, Bosley," Natalie said, dropping to her knees and gripping the radio receiver. "Tell us where you are."

October 22, Dawn
Location: A locked room, somewhere near the ocean
Status: Contemplating color schemes

Bosley was hunched next to the tiny window in his cell, holding his molar mic to his lips. His little bird friend hopped nearby, and Bosley left a morsel of bread on the windowsill for it.

Bosley bit his lip and wondered what to say. A personal message perhaps? A fond farewell. Or . . . how about something that might help the Angels find him! Oh, the little bird on the windowsill seemed to like that idea. It bobbled its head sweetly.

"I don't know where I am, really," Bosley said, glancing around his cell. "I'm in a room. The walls are white. Well, not white-white. More of a cream or an eggshell."

Bosley cocked his head and squinted at the paint job. "Vanilla. Yes, I'm going to say vanilla."

* * *

October 22, Dawn
Location: Remains of the Charles Townsend Detective
    Agency
Wardrobe: Cold sweat

The Angels gave one another sidelong looks. What was up with Bos? Why was he wasting his time with Ralph Lauren paint chips when he could be saving his own life? Was his kidnapper holding a gun to his head? Or worse?

"I can see the ocean," Bosley piped up from the crackly radio.

Alex snapped her fingers.

"Bingo," she said.

Dylan spotted a world globe in another corner. She dragged it over.

"I don't know which ocean," Bosley said. "I was blindfolded the whole time. We were flying. It might have been a couple of hours. No peanuts or anything."

Dylan glanced at the scale at the globe's base and quickly made some calculations. She looked at Alex and Natalie with a furrowed brow.

"He could be anywhere in this half of North America," she said.

Cheep, cheeeppp—coo.

Dylan glanced at the radio. That must be some bird. She shrugged and stared at the globe some more.

"Wherever it is," Bosley said, "They have really good pudding."

"What?" Dylan said, looking up again. "Pudding?"

But Natalie held up her finger and pressed her ear to the radio.

Cheeeep—coo.

Natalie's face broke into a huge smile. "That's a pygmy nuthatch!" she announced. *"Sitta Pygmaea.* They live in only one place."

Alex grinned back at Natalie and said, "Carmel."

CHAPTER

12

October 22, 6:02 am.
Location: Natalie's Ferrari
Wardrobe: Thinking caps (slightly charred)

All three Angels sat in the front seat of Natalie's Ferrari. They had scavenged gear from their car trunks—a laptop, a few wetsuits, Alex's favorite crossbow. Now they were headed north at eighty miles per hour.

"Okay," Natalie began, squinting at the road with brutal intensity. "Bosley said he could see the ocean from his window, but he didn't mention the beach."

Alex did a quick bit of mental geometry.

"Distance from shore . . . altitude above sea level," she murmured. "With a view from that angle, he must be close to the water and high up."

"A turret?" Dylan posed. "Maybe some kind of castle?"

"Hmm, left-handed waves," Natalie computed, "ten feet high . . ."

"A south-facing beach taking the swell," Dylan filled in. "Big Corona?"

"Big Corona is peaking at four feet this time of

year," Natalie said, shaking her head. "Gotta be farther north."

Alex flipped open her laptop and said, "I'll do a search and cross-index of structural features and tidal activity."

For a moment there was nothing but the sound of rushing wind and the hum of Alex's cellular modem. A few keystrokes later, Alex's face lit up.

"It *is* amazing how much you can learn off the Internet," she announced, scrolling down her screen excitedly. "I've got a lighthouse, two Colonial-era hotels, and two manor houses. One owned by the National Parks Service. One owned by . . . the Nick Xero Corporation."

"Never heard of it," Natalie blurted.

But Dylan was frowning. She turned to Alex and said, "Nick Xero. Is that with an *X* or a *Z?*"

"*X*," Alex answered.

"It's an anagram," Dylan said, slapping the dashboard.

"Hey, watch the Ferrari," Natalie said.

Dylan explained her excitement.

"Switch around the letters of *Nick Xero* and you get *Eric Knox*," she told her buds.

"Scrabble freak!" Alex cried, punching Dylan's arm gleefully. Then she began typing furiously into her laptop. In an instant, a map popped onto the screen.

"There's an old tunnel leading down to the shore," she said. "But it looks like the best way to get in undetected is a sea approach."

She clicked the computer shut and announced, "We're gonna need a boat."

"And a cover," Natalie noted. "We can't exactly pull up in the speedboat."

Dylan was stumped. Until she remembered something she'd been trying to forget for days. A bittersweet smile played around her lips as she turned to Natalie, and sighed, "Head to the marina."

October 22, 7:36 A.M.
Location: *That's Amore*, tugboat of the Chad
Question: The Chad?

Natalie and Alex were busy priming for battle. They were putting on custom-made black jumpsuits of a wicking poly-blend with flared ankles and plunging necklines. (What? A girl can't look cool when she's kicking butt?)

They were packing waterproof messenger bags with all the fighting gear they could muster.

And they were wondering just what Dylan had been thinking when she hooked up with . . . that. That googly-eyed, chinless tugboat captain with delusions of *Titanic* and a really off-key singing voice.

Alex and Natalie gaped at Chad warbling as he steered into open water. Then they looked at Dylan. They looked at Chad again. Dylan grinned and shrugged. She scurried to her partners' sides. Alex's laptop had just rebooted, and they were pondering solutions.

"We can't cut the signal from the mainframe to Bosley's laptop," Natalie observed.

"Uh-huh. It's encrypted," Alex said. "A direct transmission."

"If we could at least get a look at what Knox is seeing—piggyback on his system," Natalie mused wistfully. She turned to Alex. "Can you do that?"

Alex nodded and shrugged.

"Of course," she said. "It's not rocket science."

Natalie shot her a deadpan glare.

"I mean, it *is* rocket science," Alex admitted. "But I can do it."

Dylan was tapping one army-booted toe on the tugboat deck and glaring at her watch.

"It's almost time for Charlie's call to Bosley," she fretted.

Natalie squinted at the distant shore and joined Chad behind the wheel.

"Can't this thing go any faster?" she asked. "Please—let me drive!"

"Sorry, friend of Starfish," Chad said, "but there's only one captain on this *Love Boat.*"

After a few more agonizing minutes of puttering, the tugboat came within view of shore. Chad slowed the boat.

"I have to say, Starfish," he said, squinting happily into the sunshine, "I'm honored you've taken an interest in my work."

He turned around to face his redheaded sweetheart and gaped.

All three Angels were decked out in shiny black

Navy SEAL-style scuba gear. They had just finished fitting their masks and adjusting their oxygen calibrators. They were ready to flip back into the ocean.

"Oh," Chad whimpered, looking hurt. He gazed into Dylan's eyes behind her scuba mask.

"Was it the Chad?" he asked.

"No," Dylan said with a dazzling smile. "The Chad was great."

The last thing Dylan saw before she plunged into the water was the boat captain's goofy face dissolving into a huge grin. He pumped his fist in the air and hooted. Dylan couldn't help but giggle through her oxygen tube as she and her fellow Angels finned swiftly to a rocky beach. They landed directly beneath a tired-looking Spanish-style castle.

They squinted up at the building. There! There was a tall bell tower—a round, ivy-covered turret. Holding up her hands to make a crude protractor, Alex nodded.

"X marks the spot," she said.

And what do you know, the satellite dish that would make Knox's evil scheme possible was in the most unwieldy spot on the castle—directly on top of that turret. Alex immediately kicked into gear.

"Okay," she said to Natalie and Dylan, "if I can get to the dish in time . . ."

"I'll keep Knox occupied," Dylan volunteered.

"I'll get Bosley," Natalie said.

With a quick solidarity handslap, the Angels fanned out.

Dylan scaled the boulder-strewn cliff. When she

reached the top, she military-crawled toward the castle's courtyard. She finally had a moment alone. A chance to think. To think about what an idiot she had been.

"I don't know how to make chicken," she said, mocking Knox under her breath. "Jerk . . . Ow!"

To top it all off, she'd just banged her elbow on a mega-sharp rock. But with a stony face, Dylan pressed on.

October 22, 8:08 A.M.
Location: Eric Knox's "vacation" compound.
    Command room
Philosophy: Revenge is sweet

Vivian Wood leaned over one of several radar monitors. They were all imbedded in the craggy rock wall that lined Knox's command room. This was Knox's sanctuary, his favorite hideout—it was Gothic and dank and barren. There was nothing in the room beyond a few chairs and a host of state-of-the-art monitoring equipment and computers. Like Batman, Knox ruled over it all.

Vivian loved that about her boss. She loved his vicious power. And she loved the tinted aviator glasses he'd worn ever since offing that Angel bimbo.

She was thinking this as she scanned each screen—one, an ocean view, showed nothing but an old garbage barge. Or maybe it was a pathetic little tugboat. Whatever.

In the prisoner's room, Bosley was sitting on the edge of his cot, rocking maniacally and having a conversation with some bird. Excellent.

Vivian turned to Knox and announced, "All clear."

Nobody acknowledged her—not the three beefy henchmen loitering around the room and not the Thin Man. Of course, that weird statue of a guy never talked anyway. Knox ignored Vivian, too.

He was paying too much attention to the microcassette recorder in his hand, the one Vivian had sneaked into the agency. He held the recorder up to a speaker on his computer and hit Play.

"Corwin is the owner of Red Star Systems . . ."

It was unmistakably Charles Townsend's voice, pilfered off his speakerphone during a useless morning meeting.

But let's see if the computer can figure that out, Vivian thought, holding her breath.

The screen filled with a stream of data, a graph of colored bars, lengthening and thickening like rubber bands. Suddenly a box popped onto the screen.

"Voice print encrypted," it read. "Charles Townsend."

Vivian sighed with relief. The audio DNA identifier had worked.

"Revenge is fun," Knox purred.

He used a cable to connect a laptop to the computer. It was Bosley's laptop—stolen after Vivian had drugged his Chianti and kidnapped his unconscious body.

And it was with Bosley's laptop that Knox would log onto Red Star Systems' mainframe—and track down Charlie.

"Hello, Eric."

Knox spun around to face the voice. No one was there—until Dylan dropped from a skylight in the ceiling and landed, catlike, in front of him.

It gave Dylan only a tiny bit of satisfaction to see Knox gape at her, reeling. He'd clearly thought—hoped—that she was dead.

Knox recovered quickly. Or at least, he recovered his sarcasm quickly.

"Dylan!" he exclaimed with a sneer. "Thank goodness you're all right."

But not for long, Vivian thought. She sidled up behind the Angel.

Dylan felt the unmistakable pressure of a gun on the back of her head. She twisted slightly to see Vivian out of the corner of her eye. The babe was still wearing her hair loose, and she had on a tight, black leather bodysuit.

"You know my better half," Knox said by way of introduction.

"Figures," Dylan barked. "I meet the perfect guy and he already has his perfect gal."

A few more henchmen entered the command room to join the original crew of thugs. Vivian scowled at them and said, "I hope *somebody* remembered the duct tape."

In thirty seconds Dylan was tied to a chair and Knox was kneeling beside her, grinning smarmily.

The Thin Man glared at her and sauntered out of the room onto a balcony.

The skinny villain smoked a cigarette, gazing blankly at the ocean. A few pebbles skittered down from the roof above him and landed neatly at the Thin Man's feet.

Slowly, he stamped out his butt with the long, skinny toe of his boot. Then he glanced at the roof above him. He saw nothing, but he sensed something. Squinting, he left the balcony. Then he left the command room altogether. Better safe than sorry.

Vivian, meanwhile, had spotted a flash of activity on one of the radars. Dylan peeked beyond her and felt her heart sink.

Natalie.

Her fellow Angel had found an underground passageway and was crawling through a floor grate into the turret. She was also starring on a sick and twisted program called *Knox TV.*

"Hello, Blondie," Vivian cooed to the radar screen. She turned to Knox and announced, "Ms. Sanders's girlfriend is here."

Knox pointed to two of the thugs.

"Jimmy and Paulie," he barked. "Go check on Bosley."

But Vivian shook her head.

"Never send a man to do a woman's job," she snapped, then stalked out of the room. She'd be handling Natalie herself.

October 22, 8:26 A.M.
Location: Eric Knox's compound. Bell turret
Philosophy: Revenge may be sweet but reunion is sweeter

Natalie glanced at her watch and tried not to hyperventilate. Then she took stock of her surroundings. She was gazing up a tall, narrow bell tower with a spiral staircase hugging the cracked, stucco walls. Directly overhead, there was nothing but an enormous brass bell. Its frayed rope swung listlessly by her head.

Natalie rushed to the stairs and began taking them two at a time. When she got halfway up the turret, she saw several doors. Behind one of them lurked Bosley—Natalie was sure of it.

"Booosleeeey," she called, bounding up the stairs. "Bosley!"

When she neared the top of the turret, she heard a muffled voice.

"Natalie? Is that you?"

"Bos?"

"Natalie!"

"Bosley!" At last Natalie spotted a door with a small slot near the knob. Through that slot, she could see a familiar pair of eyes with gray bags beneath them. Good ol' Bos!

"Hi, Bosley," she enthused. She crouched to look into his frightened eyes. "I'm so glad to see you! Are you okay?"

Bosley's eyes moved up and down in a nod.

"I'm gonna get you out of here," Natalie declared. She shoved at the door and jiggled the knob. The door was solid. Without a battering ram, she'd have to re-sort to . . . a key.

But where to find it?

Natalie began tearing around the staircase land-ing, looking for loose boards, a hiding place in the crumbling wall—anything. She found nothing. She was peering beneath the banister when her cell phone rang. She scowled, whipped the phone out of a pocket in her pants leg, and flipped it open.

"Hello?" she said.

"Natalie?"

Her face lit up.

"Pete, hi!" she gushed. "How are you?"

Pete's voice was filled with uncertainty as he replied, "I'm good. I just—you said you wanted me to call."

Natalie leaned against the turret wall and gazed dreamily out a window at the top of the staircase.

"I did want you to call," she said. "I do want you to call. I mean, thank you."

"Is that Pete?" Bosley squawked through the slot in the door. "Ummm, could you ask if you can call back . . ."

"No, I wanted to call you," Pete insisted. "I really like spending time with you. I was hoping to see more of you. Y'know, maybe in one continuous block. You know, all together."

Natalie grinned. Pete was like, so into her!

"You know," she began, "it's been really crazy this week at work. It's insane, in fact—"

"Watch your back!" Bosley screamed to her.

Natalie whipped around to see two thugs barreling up the stairs. She dropped into fighting stance.

"Can you hold on a sec?" she asked Pete. She hit the mute button and tossed the phone into her left hand. Then she used her right hand to jab one guy right in the nose.

With her left thumb, she unmuted the phone and chirped, "One more sec," into the mouthpiece.

As she went into a spin, she hit mute again. She completed the turn with a roundhouse kick to the other thug's cheekbones. She thwacked the guy with her cell phone.

While he stood there, groaning, the first guy recovered and headed straight for Natalie. She held up her dukes. But just before the thug's outstretched fist could connect, Natalie made a quick parry, hopping to the left.

That left nobody in Goon #1's path but Goon #2.

The men collided with a fleshy grunt and toppled over. Over and out, that is. Screaming, they sailed through the window and tumbled into oblivion.

Natalie shook her head in annoyance. But she perked up when Bosley yelled, "Nice work, Natalie."

"Thanks, Bosley," she replied. Then she unmuted her phone.

"Sorry about that," she said to her sweetie. "Can you hold a second more?"

"You bet," Pete said.

Still holding the phone to her ear but covering the mouthpiece, Natalie crouched in front of Bosley's door.

"I like him *so* much," she confided. Bosley just rolled his eyes. Then there was Pete, piping up in her ear.

"Listen," he said, sounding a bit nervous. "Is this a bad time?"

"No, not at all," Natalie said, resuming her search for the key. She began tapping the wall, listening for hollow spots.

"You just sound distracted," Pete said.

"Well, work this week has been really busy," Natalie admitted. "It's been hard to focus."

WHOMP!

Natalie froze. Then she spun to her left. Yup—just as she'd thought. Someone had thrown an ax at her, and it had imbedded itself in the wall, missing her ear by inches.

Natalie twisted around. There was the ax tosser herself—Vivian Wood, glaring at Natalie from the landing on the opposite side of the turret.

Natalie jammed her cell phone into her waistband and glared at her foe. Then she yanked the ax out of the splintered wall and thwacked it against Bosley's doorknob, smashing the wood around it to smithereens. She kicked the door open, gave Bosley a hello wink, and tossed him the ax.

"You might need this," she said. She heard a voice squawk from her midsection. Pete!

"Are you okay, Natalie?" he said. What a sweetie. But Natalie had to keep a grip on her Wood-based rage. Ignoring Pete, she scowled at Vivian.

"Ready to rumble?" she growled.

"Let's get it on," Vivian said.

Without hesitation, both women leaped out into the vacuum between them. They collided in midair and grabbed on to each other, falling as one. The door to the turret fell with them.

For a few brief moments they got hung up on an unfortunately placed beam. Then, with angry screams, they plummeted to the bottom of the turret. They landed with a thud and lay on the floor, stunned and unable to move.

CHAPTER

13

October 22, 8:39 A.M.
Location: The bell tower roof
Metaphor: Mouse . . . and cat

Alex felt as if she'd been climbing for an eon. But at last, she was here—at the roof of the turret. She hoisted herself and her bag of gear over the edge of the roof and scanned the area. There in the middle of the roof was the structure that sheltered the bell and its raggedy rope. And—aha—inside it was Alex's prey: A Nera satellite phone and Trimble GPS unit. These gadgets were Knox's connection to Red Star's satellites and thus, to Charlie.

Alex skittered across the roof to the little space-communication station and yanked out the main cable, splicing open its rubber casing with the all-purpose knife she always kept on her person.

As she had expected, a cornucopia of tiny, colored wires spilled out of the cable. Alex pulled out some small pliers and got to work connecting Knox's system to her laptop.

"Red wire . . ." she muttered, ". . . blue wire."

She was sweating through the complex machinations when a tiny black-and-yellow bird darted at the back of her head.

"What the—" Alex blurted, spinning around.

The momentum tumbled her right into the Thin Man! He was bearing down on her, leering and swinging that silly white cane of his.

Alex immediately attacked, realizing as she did, that if that pygmy nuthatch hadn't startled her, she might have been a goner.

But she didn't have time to think about that now. She was in the thick of combat.

And the Thin Man was good.

He clipped the side of Alex's head with a blow that made her see stars. In an instant, she'd recovered and thwacked him in the chest with her elbow. When he hunched over with a grunt, she ramrodded his forehead with her knee.

The Thin Man countered with a sidelong chop to Alex's ribcage. She went with it, spinning around to finish with a roundhouse kick so brutal, it knocked him off his feet.

Alex relaxed for just an instant, slumping against the bell chamber. She thought she had him.

She thought wrong.

Before she could plot her next move, the Thin Man did a reverse handspring, popping from his back onto his feet. Then he ripped at his cane. Alex realized it was a sheath for a skinny, razor-sharp sword.

He took a swipe at her neck.

Alex ducked and the sword thwacked the bell rope. From her crouched position, Alex pounced, grabbing the Thin Man's skinny torso in a death crunch.

As the Thin Man flailed around the roof with Alex clinging to him like a poison tick, she was dimly aware of the almost-severed bell rope snapping.

October 22, 8:43 A.M.
Location: The turret. Ground floor
Status: Reaching out and touching someone

The bell was falling.

Natalie and Vivian had just stumbled to their feet. Natalie, though still shaky from the force of her tumble through the turret, was in full fighting stance.

That's when she heard a slight whistling noise over her head. She looked up and gasped. The bell, a three-ton brass monstrosity, was bearing down upon them.

Natalie took a running leap and dove out of the turret's main entrance. She was vaguely aware of Vivian right behind her.

Now Natalie was acutely aware of the wide swath of steps that led up to that door, because she was pitching down them in painful twists and somersaults. Finally, she landed on a walled terrace— one that teetered on the edge of the cliff and provided a dazzling ocean view. Natalie jumped to her feet.

Vivian landed about fifteen feet away and did the same.

Vivian leaped into the air and landed a brutal kick to Natalie's shoulder. Then she started throwing punches.

Naturally, Natalie responded with her own arsenal of kung fu moves. But the witch was surprisingly good. Natalie grunted as Vivian's pointy little fist landed on her cheekbone.

She countered with a sucker punch to Vivian's gut. Then Vivian landed a blow to Natalie's sternum that forced every oxygen molecule out of her lungs.

Zeroing in for the finish, Vivian hoisted the turret door and hurled it at Natalie. Natalie scrambled to recover and demolished the door with a kick. Her cell phone popped out of her waistband and bounced across the stone floor.

Then Vivian did the unthinkable—she co-opted Natalie's cell. Scooping it off the floor, she put it to her ear and breathed, "Is this the famous Charlie?"

Natalie could faintly hear her honey responding, "It's Pete." And she could *totally* hear the tone of his voice—he was confused and he was hurt.

As if Vivian cared. She pulled the cell phone from her ear and gave it a sneer. Then she tossed it over her shoulder . . . *and off the cliff.*

Natalie jumped to her feet and gasped. She felt her eyes bulge with rage.

"You creep!" she screamed. "I *like* that guy!"

Vivian screwed her face into a mock pout, then wiped an imaginary tear from her eye.

That's it, Natalie thought. She's meat.

October 22, 8:59 A.M.
Location: The command room
Wardrobe: The bondage look

Dylan could see a vein throbbing in Knox's temple as he kneeled before her. She had an urge to lunge at him, but the ropes binding her wrists behind her chair back were too tight to give any leeway. And the last thing Dylan needed right now was a dislocated shoulder.

Of course, she began to reconsider when she heard the detestable words that came out of Knox's tight lips.

"You know, Dylan," he mused, "under different circumstances, I think we could have made a great couple."

"Yeah," Dylan said dryly, "if you didn't shoot me out of a window and try to kill everyone I love, I think we could have had a chance."

Knox grinned creepily.

"Can you keep a secret?" he simpered. "You have to promise never to tell a living soul."

"What?" Dylan spat. "That you're disgusting?"

Knox threw his head back and laughed. Then he leered at Dylan.

"You have the fullest, sweetest, most luscious lips I

have ever kissed," he declared. Then he slapped a piece of duct tape over Dylan's mouth. In the reflection of one of the radar screens, Dylan could see that Knox had painted a pair of cartoonish red lips on the tape. What a sicko.

She was even more appalled when he leaned in and planted a violent kiss on those garish lips.

Dylan flinched and shook her head. But then a shrill sound made her freeze.

Bleep, bleep.

It was a cell phone. It was *Bosley's* cell phone, which was stashed securely in Knox's pocket.

Dylan's eyes flashed to a clock on the wall. It was 9:00 on the dot. That was Charlie.

"I'm sorry, Dylan," Knox sneered, "but I just have to take this call."

He strode to his computer and quickly entered in the voice ID activator and satellite tracking command. Then he flipped open the cell, hitting the speaker button so Dylan could hear every word of her beloved boss's downfall.

"Mr. Bosley's phone," Knox said cheerfully. "Eric Knox speaking."

"Mr. Knox, this is Charles Townsend," said the familiar, gravelly voice. Dylan's stomach clenched and she struggled to yell through her duct tape gag, to yank her hands free of their ropes. Would these be the last words she'd ever hear Charlie utter?

"Mr. Townsend," Knox enthused. "How are you? *We're* all down at the beach, having mimosas. Can you join us?"

"I'll take a rain check, Eric," Charlie said evenly. "I've made other plans. Is Bosley there?"

Knox mockingly pretended to look for Bosley in the shadowy corners of the command room. Then he cheerfully replied, "Bosley went to the men's room. He should be right back—no, wait—here he comes."

Knox looked like he was holding in a fit of giggles as he said, "Can you hold on just a second longer, sir? Bosley? He's coming. He's on his way, sir."

Dylan watched Knox hunch over the computer screen. The audio DNA identifier had recognized Charlie's voice over the phone. Now the satellite was closing in on his location. Dylan could see a distant picture of earth, zooming in quickly. Now it was showing North America. Now the West Coast.

Dylan's eyes bugged out. Charlie had no idea he was being hunted like a dog.

"Not a problem," Charlie said to Knox patiently.

As the computer continued to zero in on Charlie—now it was on Southern California—Knox put on an apologetic tone.

"Oh, nope," he said. "Not him. Jeez, I have to get new glasses. Sorry, is there a message?"

"Just tell him I called as planned," Charlie said.

"Gotcha," Knox answered coldly. He snapped the phone shut and turned to Dylan.

"That man has a beautiful telephone voice," he announced. Then he mashed another bruising kiss onto Dylan's gagged mouth—and ripped the duct tape away.

Dylan gasped, sucking in a great gulp of oxygen.

Then she glared at Knox, who was bustling around the command room, gathering weapons and other supplies.

"Bad news, baby," he said. "I have to leave. I gotta go torture and kill your boss."

He snapped his fingers and a quartet of thugs lumbered into the room. Knox gestured flippantly at Dylan and said, "You guys like angel cake?"

October 22, 9:06 A.M.
Location: Turret roof
Status: Multitasking

The Thin Man's swipe at the bell rope had unbalanced him and given Alex the upper hand in their hand-to-hand combat.

At this very moment, she had him in the perfect position to administer her famous knuckle-punch. But just as she was about to lay it on him, a blip caught the corner of Alex's eye. Something was happening on her laptop.

She averted her eyes for a split second. It was long enough to see that the unthinkable had happened—Knox had a lockdown on Charlie's position. Her beloved bossman was just north of Paradise Cove. She could even make out the fuzzy satellite picture of the site—a crescent-shaped beach, a small cabin, some curiously tall rock formations jutting into the Pacific surf.

This was also long enough for the Thin Man to wrest back control of their fight.

He lunged at her, swiping his leg behind her knees.

Alex gasped with surprise as she felt her balance leave her.

She fell to the roof, but for some reason, she didn't stop when she hit the Spanish tiles. Alex heard the sickening sound of timbers breaking and moldering plaster crumbling. The roof opened up beneath her, and Alex plunged through it. She was dimly aware of her gear bag—with all her weaponry and tools uselessly tucked inside—falling with her.

She landed on a terrace, one of many attached to this strangely built Gothic turret. It jutted out from the tower over the rocky beach a hundred feet below. It also loomed over the lower courtyard, where Alex spotted Natalie and Vivian duking it out.

She heard the Thin Man drop to the terrace behind her. She spun around and attacked once again. But in her head, she was silently cheering on her friend.

"Get her, Nat!" Alex muttered through gritted teeth.

October 22, 9:10 A.M.
Location: The turret. Lower courtyard
Motto: Hell hath no fury . . .

With a high-pitched war whoop, Natalie leaped into the air and kicked Vivian full-on in the chest. Natalie began to throw punches without strategy but with plenty of muscle. She would pummel this boyfriend-bashing witch into oblivion.

"Do you have any idea," Natalie screeched as her fists flailed, "how difficult it is to find a quality man in Los Angeles?"

She clamped Vivian's sneering face in her fingers. Vivian writhed and clawed, but Natalie's strength had become superhuman.

"What you did was just *wrong*," Natalie spat. With that, she gave Vivian a massive head butt. She watched with vicious satisfaction as Vivian's eyes fluttered shut. The villain slumped to the courtyard floor.

As Natalie kicked Vivian's unconscious body out of her way, she heard a thud above her. Peering up to a terrace that jutted out of the turret, she spotted Alex—Alex with a chain around her neck, being choked by the Thin Man.

October 22, 9:17 A.M.
Location: The command room
Homage: Michael Jackson

Each of the Angels had her favorite tool of the trade. Alex's was her trusty crossbow. Natalie's was her Pokémon decoder ring. And Dylan's was her long-lost father's Zippo lighter, a formerly brass-plated number that had been worn to a soft sheen.

Why was she thinking about such a trinket when she was tied to a chair and facing down a quartet of bruisers?

Because one of them had added insult to injury. He'd reached into her pocket and filched that lighter.

"Don't take my lighter," Dylan warned.

The thug laughed at her, then flicked open the Zippo. He was just touching the flame to his cigarette when Dylan made good on her warning. She gave a great heave and lifted her body—and the chair she was tied to—into the air. She used the downward momentum to shatter the spindle between her chair legs. Her feet just happened to have been tied to that spindle.

She shot her freed leg out and kicked the lighter— still flaming—out of the henchman's hand. Then she slid the chair backward and caught the lighter behind her back. She twisted it in her fingers until she could feel the heat of the fire near her wrist. If she couldn't break the ropes that bound her to this chair, she'd burn them.

The she turned a cocky grin on the thugs.

"Wait," she ordered as they began to loom toward her.

"I've got something to tell you," she said tauntingly. "I just want you to know when this is over, every one of you will be laid out on the floor and I'm going to moonwalk out of here."

"Uh-huh," one of the thugs said, rolling his eyes and cracking his knuckles. "Are you finished?"

"No," Dylan said with another sly grin. She looked at two of the thugs. "You're not listening. See, first *you're* going to help me out of this chair. Then I'm going to play a little leapfrog with you before I break *his* nose."

She tossed her head toward one of the other bruisers.

"Then that bucket behind me has *your* face all over it," she told another.

Finally, she turned to the last of the four goons and said, "And you . . . we'll improvise. It'll be fun."

All that talk had been a stalling tactic. But the tactic was tapped out, and the lighter had barely begun to singe the thick ropes around her wrists.

So Dylan put on an even cockier face and informed her foes, "And since my trusty lighter won't work, I'm going to do all this with my hands tied behind my back."

"Get her," the first goon growled.

Dylan pitched herself backward. She hit the floor hard, and the chair splintered into a dozen pieces. Before Goon #1 could react, Dylan pulled her knees to her chest and brought her hands in front of her. Then she decked him. The blow left the thug in a pile on the floor.

Goon #2 raced toward her, his arms outstretched. As predicted, Dylan planted a foot on the unconscious thug's shoulder and vaulted herself over his rag doll body. She collided with the second guy in midair and felt her forehead connect with his nose. As he screamed in pain, the thug's nose broke with a squelching noise and a spurt of blood.

Goon #3 was headed her way. Dylan paused. She decided to psych him out with her favorite yoga pose.

"King Kong Palm," she announced, readying her hands for a flurry of deadly punches. She saw the thug's face twist with confusion. It delayed him just enough to allow her to launch into a series of back flips. On one of the rotations, she slipped her foot through the handle of the bucket she'd seen earlier. When she flipped for the last time, she used the centrifugal force to fling the bucket at Goon #3. It hit his face with a clunk, and he catapulted backward in a dead faint.

"And you . . ." Dylan had said to Goon #4, "we'll improvise."

How about another yoga pose, Dylan mused. She faced the final guy and floated one leg in front of her, her toe pointed gracefully.

"Buddha on Lotus," she said.

The thug, eyeing his prone buddies suspiciously, inched toward her. Dylan remained on one leg, looking beatific.

Finally, he leaped at her.

Faster than a snake's tongue, Dylan flicked her leg out, landing her toe on his collarbone. As she knew she would, she hit a nerve that renders the entire body temporarily paralyzed when the proper pressure is applied. With a stunned groan, the final goon sank to the floor.

My, my, Dylan thought, I'm almost winded. She surveyed the pile of bodies around her and laughed a dry, little laugh. Then, shaking her hips in triumph, she did a celebratory moonwalk out of the room. In the hall she caught sight of a familiar, craggy face.

Bosley.

"Dylan!" he cried. He gaped at her arms. "Oh my gosh, you're all tied up. Let me help you."

Bosley rushed to her side and used his ax to cut the ropes on Dylan's hands.

"Thanks, Bos," Dylan cooed, relieved to see him alive and well.

"The girls are upstairs," he replied breathlessly.

CHAPTER

14

October 22, 9:31 A.M.
Location: The turret. Upper terrace
Status: Double trouble

With Vivian Wood slumped at her feet, Natalie was free to bail out her bud, who was just a few seconds away from being sliced and diced by the Thin Man.

"Alex!" she called as she bounded up the steps toward the upper terrace.

But just as Natalie reached the top of the stairs, Vivian—fully revived and out for revenge—vaulted over the terrace banister. She must have climbed up the ivy clinging to the side of the turret.

Screaming in rage, Vivian slammed Natalie into the wall.

The commotion distracted the Thin Man enough to make him loosen his grip on Alex. She lunged for a nearby rock and used all her strength to thunk it onto the skinny creep's head. The blow sent him sprawling, and Alex leaped to her feet in fighting stance.

Behind her, Natalie shoved Vivian away with a

massive burst of strength. Vivian sailed across the terrace, landing in a heap next to the Thin Man.

In two shakes both villains had leaped to their feet. They stood side by side, snarling at their foes.

Natalie rushed to Alex's side and lifted her fists.

It was a four-way face-off.

Make that five. Dylan had run up the turret's spiral interior stairs and emerged at the upper terrace door. It took her but an instant to size up the sitch. Her brown eyes flickered from the two bad guys to her fellow Angels to a long chain slithering across the terrace floor. She followed the chain to its source—a rusty old cannon.

Dylan smiled. Oh, for a challenge.

Diving to the floor, she grabbed the chain, whirled it around her head twice and threw. Back in her rodeo days, they hadn't called Dylan the Hog-Tyin' Hottie for nothing. Her lassoing skills were still excellent.

The chain landed in a loop around the evil duo. Then all three Angels ran at the cannon and gave it a massive kick.

With a rusty groan, the thousand-pound armament rolled to the edge of the terrace, crumbling the banister.

Then it fell off, taking Vivian Wood and the Thin Man down with it.

The Angels ran to the edge of the balcony and peered over. The villains were about ten feet below them, white-lipped, trembling and dangling from the chain, which had caught on a boulder jutting from the cliff face.

One false move, and the two might go plummeting to the rocky beach. In other words, the Angels had them right where they wanted them.

Eric Knox was another story entirely.

That much was clear when the psychopath's two-seater helicopter—with a loaded missile launcher on each skid—rose from the beach. It was as if the chopper were rising from the pits of hell, blasting the Angels with hot wind.

Shielding their eyes from the cyclone of grit that swirled around them, the Angels watched Knox size up the situation. There were the Angels, and there were his comrades, trapped, a few feet away.

If he took out the Angels, he'd have to take out his flunkies, too.

Dylan watched Knox press two fingers to his lips and then to the window, giving Vivian a little wave.

Then she saw him press the rocket launch button.

Giving her comrades a quick, go-for-it glance, Dylan counted to three. They raced to the edge of the terrace . . . and jumped.

October 22, 9:45 A.M.
Location: The turret. Lower terrace
Status: Alive and intact

As they landed on the lower terrace, rolling violently on the stone floor, the Angels felt the heat of the explosion above them. When the dust cleared, they squinted upward.

Knox had blown the upper terrace—indeed, the entire top half of the turret—to kingdom come.

With it had gone Vivian Wood and the Thin Man.

Dylan couldn't help but feel a wrench in her gut. Knox's brutality stunned even her.

But this was no time to be maudlin. Eric Knox knew Charlie's position. They had to get to Charlie before Knox did.

But how?

Screeeeccch!

With a spray of gravel and some really erratic steering, a tricked-out, blue Bronco convertible skidded up to the Angels, with Bosley behind the wheel!

"Get in!" he called with a grin.

As Alex was racing to leap into the vehicle, she spotted her crossbow among the rubble of the turret. It must have been launched from her gear bag in the explosion and fallen to the lower terrace. What luck! Alex scooped up the weapon and tumbled into the Bronco just as Bosley peeled out. There was no time for Natalie to jump into the driver's seat, so she rode shotgun and steered while Bosley put the pedal to the metal.

Remembering Charlie's placement on her laptop, Alex ordered, "Head north! Just past Paradise Cove."

"That's Charlie's cabin," Bosley yelled as Natalie skidded them onto a dirt road. "The sanctum sanctorum. His hideout."

Natalie almost lost her grip on the wheel. Alex almost dropped her crossbow. Dylan almost swallowed her gum. They all gaped at Bosley.

"You've seen it?" Alex demanded.

"You've seen Charlie?" Dylan blurted.

"I am his trusted friend and employee," Bosley stated. He was evading, big-time.

"You've met Charlie?" Natalie squeaked.

"Define *met*," Bosley said.

"You've seen him with your own eyes," Dylan declared impatiently.

"No . . ." Bosley hemmed and hawed. "I saw his hand! About nine years ago, I delivered some papers to his cabin. I left them against the door. As I was driving away, out of the rearview, I saw him pick them up."

"Could've been anyone's hand," Alex scoffed. Then she turned her attention back to the helicopter. Natalie and Bosley's excellent joint driving had brought them to a point almost below the speeding chopper. Alex stood in the back of the Bronco and took careful aim.

"Let's see if I can win a teddy bear," she called. She shot her crossbow. She'd attached a long and sturdy cable to the barbed arrow, and it unfurled beside her with a zip.

Aaaaannnd . . . thunk. Yes! Alex had scored a direct hit. The arrow was lodged in the underbelly of the chopper and the cable was trailing behind it like a wild serpent.

"Do you mind driving, Bos?" Natalie yelled.

"Now?" Bosley squealed.

"Now!" Natalie barked. Bosley grabbed the wheel. Then Natalie did a flip into the back of the Bronco and grabbed the cable.

Dylan got a grip next.

Finally, Alex caught the cable's tail end.

The trio exploded out of the Bronco. They flew away like, well, Angels, trailing gracefully behind the speeding helicopter.

Bosley gazed up at his girls. A tear of pride glistened in the corner of his eye. Then he glanced at the road. Except, there wasn't any more road. In about twenty feet it ended in a sheer drop off the cliff.

Bosley screamed and slammed his foot on the brake. The Bronco skidded and bucked like, well, a bronco, and finally skittered to a halt, teetering on the edge of the cliff.

Sweating and straining, Bosley gingerly lifted himself out of the truck and fell to the ground, just as the Bronco tumbled with a thunderous crash, deep into the canyon.

Bosley gazed up at the Angels, who now looked like nothing but a speck trailing the thundering chopper. He gave a little wave.

"Vaya con Dios, my darlings," he murmured.

CHAPTER

15

October 22, 10:13 A.M.
Location: Airborne below Eric Knox's two-seater chopper
Wardrobe: Sticky fingers

The Angels trailed behind the helicopter. They were flying so swiftly they could barely gulp oxygen out of the rushing wind, could barely keep their eyes open to see. Painfully, they crawled up the cable, hand over hand, one at a time, until each woman was hanging from the chopper's skids.

They exchanged glances, but they didn't speak. This mission was too treacherous and too terrifying to chat through.

For Charlie, it's worth it, Dylan thought fiercely as the wind blasted a hank of her red hair across her face.

"We're gonna make this happen," Alex muttered to herself, "or die trying."

She peeked beneath the helicopter's body and realized they had only minutes to do it. She could spot Charlie's cabin in the distance—she recognized the little house, the unusual rock formations and the crescent-shaped beach from the satellite picture she'd seen on her laptop.

Alex shot her compadres a thumbs-up. Then each Angel fanned out.

October 22, 10:26 A.M.
Location: Knox's chopper. Cockpit
Mission: Payback

Dylan crept along the chopper's skid, fighting madly against the whipping wind. Finally, she was just outside the cockpit. She breathed deeply. Thoughts of Charlie flitted across her mind. Then she gritted her teeth and swung into Knox's view.

Was it just Dylan's imagination, or was Knox singing when she crashed through the chopper door? No matter now—the minute she was inside the cockpit, Dylan shut him up with a brutal punch to the jaw.

Knox blinked, shaking his head. He was stunned. And then he was enraged. Keeping one hand on the steering wheel, he struck back at Dylan, landing a stinging blow to her temple.

Dylan's legs were trembling with the urge to round-kick Knox right out of this bird. But in the tiny, cramped space of the cockpit, most of her fave kung fu moves were useless.

So she screamed and lunged at his face, scratching, slapping, and clawing.

Knox was ready for her. He shoved her hard, sending her sprawling and banging her head.

October 22, 10:27 A.M.
Location: Knox's chopper. Right missile launcher
Motto: When in doubt, always fall back on rocket science

Alex whipped a bungee cord out of her pants pocket and lashed herself to the chopper's skid. There was no way she could fall off now.

Of course, if anything dire happened, there was no way she could escape, either.

Alex shook the thought away and opened up a circuit board beneath the missile tube. Feverishly, she began yanking wires, then reconnecting them. She adjusted a sensor. She futzed with the flux manifold. Then she did a few other things that nobody, save a few, select NASA scientists, could possibly understand.

October 22, 10:29 A.M.
Location: Knox's chopper. Beneath the tail
Theme song: She floats through the air, with the greatest
    of ease . . .

Natalie sighed. Naturally, Knox would own a KS-7, a two-seater chopper. It was a great little helicopter, but for Natalie's needs, it was highly inconvenient.

Resigned, she grabbed for the cable trailing from the copter's underbelly. She tied it around her waist, binding it with a C-clamp from her jumpsuit pocket. Then she did an inverted dive off the skid.

Catching the bar with her fingertips, she swung off in a wide arc, twisting in midair until she caught the chopper by the tail. She wrapped her long legs around the tail, crossing her ankles. Then she let go with her hands.

She was hanging from a speeding helicopter thousands of feet above sea level. Upside down. With her knees.

Now for the hard part.

Natalie located the control panel and flipped it open. Fishing around inside, she located a cable—the steering cable. Grinning, she grabbed the cable and gave it a good yank.

Nothing happened.

She pulled on it again.

It was unmovable.

That's when Natalie started to sweat.

October 22, 10:30 A.M.
Location: Knox's chopper. Cockpit
Battle: Steel will against iron will

Knox was jabbing at Dylan with one hand. With the other, he released the steering wheel to reach for the handgun he had stuffed into his waistband.

Dylan socked Knox in the gut and went for the gun herself.

Elbowing her out of the way, Knox grabbed the steering wheel again before the bird went out of control. And then he spotted it.

Charlie's cabin.

He was close enough to get a shot at it.

Dylan saw Knox go ruddy with delight. His breath quickened. He was reaching toward the dashboard—and the missile launch command button.

October 22, 10:31 A.M.
Location: Beneath the chopper tail
Status: Desperate

Natalie gritted her teeth and strained every bicep, tricep, and deltoid she had. The steering cable was going nowhere.

She'd have to enlist the rest of her muscles, too.

Natalie unwrapped her long legs from around the chopper's tail and planted a foot on each side of the control panel. Then she grabbed the cable again.

She flung her body backward, pulling with superhuman strength.

In an instant, the frayed cable was in her hands.

And Natalie was falling through the air.

October 22, 10:31 A.M.
Location: Cockpit
Status: Desperate

Dylan karate-chopped Knox's outstretched arm, slamming it away from the missile launch button.

Knox roared with rage and grabbed Dylan by the

back of the neck. He slammed her head into the dash, leaving a bloody welt on her forehead. Dylan blinked hard and struggled not to sink into unconsciousness. She gazed at Knox dully as he tried to guide the chopper closer to Charlie's cabin.

And then Knox was cursing.

He was jerking the steering wheel back and forth.

He was screaming through gritted teeth.

The steering was gone.

At the same time, Dylan heard a frantic beeping coming from the dashboard. She glanced at a screen with target crosshairs on it. It was blinking. A caption flashed: Target Position Locked. Fire Now.

Knox gave Dylan a smarmy sneer. Then he thrust out his finger and hit the button.

The screen began to flash: Missile Launched. Missile Launched. Missile Launched.

October 22, 10:31 A.M.
Location: Right missile launcher
Status: Desperate

Alex was attaching the last wire to the last circuit. Her fingers trembled as she wrapped the tiny wire around a minuscule screw. Where were her pliers?

Finally, she linked the metal on metal as crudely as she could.

Bzzzzttt.

The missile was firing up.

Alex raised her hands to avoid electrical burns. She began struggling to unloose her bungee cord.

BZZZZZZTTTTT.

In another second Alex would literally be toast. Hopping into midair, she watched the bungee slacken. She gave it a shake and unleashed the hook that held it in place.

FWWWWOOOOM.

The missile launched.

And Alex went into a free fall.

October 22, 10:31 A.M.
Location: Cockpit
Status: Still desperate

Dylan watched the missile stream away from the chopper in a plume of blue smoke.

She felt all of the emotions of the past few days well up inside her: her misguided ardor for Knox, her undying loyalty to Charlie, her passionate devotion to her fellow Angels.

Then all those feelings transformed. Into rage. Into strength.

"Nooooo!" Dylan screamed. She hauled back and punched Knox with a force she'd never achieved before.

Knox's face was bloodied. It was bruised. And, unbelievably, it was still smiling—an evil, vengeful, psychotic grin.

Dylan glimpsed that hateful grin for only an instant, because Natalie appeared at her shattered window, swinging in like Tarzan's Jane on a vine.

She grabbed Dylan, yanking her out of the chopper.

Then Natalie unclamped the cable around her waist. She began falling toward the ocean.

Dylan fell with her.

Nearby, Alex was already plummeting.

In midair the Angels' eyes met. And then they gazed at Charlie's cabin. The missile was hissing toward it at the speed of sound.

Good-bye Charlie, Dylan thought.

Adios, bossman, Natalie thought. Tears welled up in her eyes.

Hope this works, Alex thought, holding her breath.

The missile began to turn around.

Dylan and Natalie gasped.

"Yes!" Alex screamed.

The bomb did a complete 180. Then it headed for Knox's chopper.

Through the cracked window of the cockpit, Dylan could hear Knox's raspy voice screaming in disbelief and terror.

The missile connected with the chopper in a massive fireball while the Angels floated through the air, descending toward the cool, blue Pacific. As they fell, they could feel the heat of the explosion rushing over their heads.

They hit the water.

The burning helicopter plummeted after them.

The Angels swam for the ocean floor. When they hit the sand, they looked up. All they could see was the blurry orange glow of Armageddon.

They hovered beneath the surface for as long as they could before shooting upward, stretching for oxygen and hoping for the best.

By the time they came up for air, blinking salt water out of their eyes, the burnt chopper husk had begun to sink. As the last bit of the cockpit dunked beneath the waves, the flames were extinguished with a loud hiss.

Dylan looked at Natalie, who looked at Alex. They blinked gravely. Then, one by one, they broke into grins. They were alive. They were unhurt. And they were still Angels.

October 22, 10:38 A.M.
Location: Charlie's beach
Wardrobe: That classic Angel look

The angels swam to shore. Three abreast, they hiked out of the waves onto the beach. Their hair was slicked back, their T-shirts were plastered to their torsos, and their jumpsuits were in shreds.

They fell to their knees, coughing and breathing hard. When they'd caught their breath, Natalie gave Alex a playful look.

"Recalibrated the missile's sensor grid to track to the chopper's thermal signature?" she asked.

Alex nodded. "Rocket science," she said with a shrug.

They laughed, but Dylan was somber. She was gazing up the beach at the small cabin. It was built of weathered, soft-gray shingles and had a little porch. A hammock hung beneath a palm tree. From the chimney, peaceful little puffs of smoke wafted into the air.

Natalie was the first to say what they were all thinking.

"Charlie!" she gasped. "Come on."

The trio scrambled across the sand.

"What do you think he looks like?" Dylan breathed as she fixed her eyes on the cabin.

"Easy," Natalie said, ticking off the qualities she'd always imagined in their elusive honcho. "Sixty, tall, well-built. Always wearing a tux."

"No way," Alex said, looking dreamy. "Younger. Fifty. Incredibly athletic."

"And maybe," Natalie added, "just a teeny bit of cologne—and a tan."

Alex shot Dylan a deadpan look. Then she poked Natalie in the ribs.

"He's not George Hamilton," she scoffed.

Before they knew it, they were standing at Charlie's front door. Dylan was suddenly very aware of Natalie's salt-matted hair and Alex's shredded jumpsuit. She wiped sandy smudges from her own cheeks and tried to run her fingers through her tangled hair.

"Do I look okay?" she asked worriedly.

Alex and Natalie checked out the disheveled Dylan.

"Frankly, no," Alex blurted. All three burst into nervous laughter.

Finally there was nothing left to do but meet the bossman.

"Should we knock?" Alex whispered.

Dylan shook her head and tried the knob. It was unlocked. Holding her breath, she opened the door. The Angels peeked inside, then entered the little cabin—it was all rustic pine furniture, beautiful leather couches, and artifacts that the Angels' trained eyes recognized as priceless bits of history from Africa, South America, and the Middle East.

They crept into the room and looked around.

Nobody was there.

Dylan's heart was sinking when that voice—that familiar, gravelly, wonderful voice—piped up from outside the cabin.

"Hello, Angels," Charlie said.

All three women spun around and rushed out the door.

"Charlie?" they blurted en masse.

But nobody was there. Nobody except a small, cream-colored box, with a speckled plastic circle on its front. A speakerphone sitting on a little table.

"Charlie . . ." Dylan said, disappointed and elated and breathless all at the same time.

"We're so happy to see you," Natalie gushed. "Well, not, see you, but . . . well, you're okay!"

"I'm just fine, Angels," Charlie answered. Then he asked his standard question. "Mission accomplished?"

Dylan and her compadres exchanged proud glances.

"I think the client was impressed with our work," Dylan said dryly.

"As am I," Charlie said. "How about a vacation, Angels?"

October 23, Happy Hour
Location: A beach somewhere in Maui
Wardrobe: Bikinis and leis

The Angels barely had had time to get home and pack before Charlie spirited them away to Hawaii.

Now Dylan sank her toes into the warm island sand and lounged on a beach chair, taking a lazy sip from a tropical smoothie. Alex was sunning herself in a tiny bikini while Natalie read a magazine, nursed some guava juice, and toyed with her lei. There were sighs of contentment all around, even from Bosley, who was well-protected from the tropical sun by a goofy grass hat and dab of white zinc oxide on his nose. He was slurping a bright blue daiquiri.

When Bos's green cell phone rang, the Angels sat up, gazing at it expectantly.

"Right, Charlie," Bosley said into the cell. Then he hit the speakerphone button and laid it on the beach towel.

"Great work, Angels," Charlie's familiar, scratchy voice said. "I'm sure you're eager to hear about the missing pieces in the Eric Knox case."

Dylan caught her breath and sat up, staring intently at the cell phone.

"Eric Knox was born John McCadden," Charlie explained. "It seems his life's mission was to bring me down. His father was in my Army Intel unit. He was working as a double agent, and when he got found out, he was killed by the other side."

Dylan sighed sadly. "I guess that's not the story Knox heard."

Bosley sat up straighter, too. He puffed out his chest.

"I just want you to know, Charlie, even though I was *cruelly* seduced, mercilessly pistol-whipped, and wrongfully detained under appallingly primitive conditions, I really enjoyed this assignment and can't wait to get back to work."

The Angels exchanged mischievous glances. Natalie covered her mouth to keep from laughing out loud. Instead, she piped up, "Me, too. *If* we had an agency to work out of . . ."

"I already have a team rebuilding the office," Charlie said reassuringly. "It'll be better than new by the time you get back. Enjoy your vacation, Angels."

"Thank you, Charlie," the threesome replied in their typical just-for-Charlie singsong.

Could this get any better?

Well, maybe.

Dylan looked at the speakerphone. As always, she pictured Charlie's imaginary face rather than a piece of equipment with numbers and an antenna.

"Any chance you'll be joining us, Charlie?" she asked quietly.

Calmly, coolly, as always, Charlie replied, "I'd love to, Angels, but I have some precious treasures to watch over."

"But how will we ever know you really exist, Charlie, if you don't come down here and join us?" Natalie asked.

"Faith, Angels," Charlie responded. "It's called faith."

Then he clicked off and was gone.

October 23, Happy Hour
Location: A beach somewhere in Maui
Wardrobe: Incognito

A slim, silver-haired man walked next to the ocean, feeling the warm Hawaiian sand beneath his bare feet. In one hand, he held a frosty drink with an umbrella in it. In the other, he had a cell phone.

"Faith, Angels," he said into the cell. "It's called Faith."

He closed his phone and kept walking.

But then the man paused and turned slightly. He gazed up the beach at three gorgeous young women—a playful blond, a serious dark-haired beauty, and a mesmerizing redhead.

Suddenly, the redhead turned, as if under a spell, and looked straight at him. For a moment she locked eyes with the man. He tipped his hat, and then he sauntered away.

October 23, Happy Hour
Location: A beach somewhere in Maui
Status: Moving on

Dylan gazed across the beach. She was drawn, as if
by a magnet, to the tanned, silver-haired man standing about a hundred feet away.

Their eyes locked.

Dylan felt a peace wash over her. She'd never seen
this slim stranger, yet there was something utterly familiar about him.

She glanced away quickly and shook her head. Was
that who she thought it was? When she gazed down
the beach again, the man—Charlie?—had disappeared.

Dylan felt no regret. No typical emptiness. She
smiled wryly at the dormant cell phone on the beach
towel. Then she winked at Alex and Natalie and
raised her smoothie glass.

"To Charlie," she called.

"To Charlie!" echoed Alex, Natalie, and Bosley.

Clink. Their glasses met. They sipped. Then they
laughed uproariously as Bosley fumbled and sprayed
his blue daiquiri all over them. Still laughing, they
chased him into the surf.

Why not laugh? They were alive. They were unhurt. And they were still, would always be, Angels.

About the Author

ELIZABETH LENHARD is the author of Pocket Books' *Clueless: Bettypalooza* and the novelization *Dudley Do-Right*. She has also written horror and sci-fi thrillers for young readers. A former staff writer for the *Atlanta Journal-Constitution*, she is now a contributing dining critic at *Chicago* magazine and a columnist at *Swoon*. She lives and writes in the shadow of Wrigley Field, in Chicago.